The General's Women

Valley & McElhatten

THE GENERAL'S WOMEN
... a presentation in dialogue

Interviews • Letters • Poems • Diaries
Explore
General Douglas MacArthur's Loves

Researched and Created by
David J. Valley
Betty McElhatten

Published by
The Sektor Company
San Diego, California

Valley & McElhatten

THE GENERAL'S WOMEN
... a presentation in dialogue

Published by
The Sektor Company
Post Office Box 501005
San Diego, CA 92150

Library of Congress Catalog Number
2004096584

Author's email:
dvalley1@san.rr.com
mcbetty1@aol.com

The General's Women - First Edition

ISBN: 0-9678175-6-0

Printed in the United States of America

TABLE OF CONTENTS

T A B L E O F C O N T E N T S

Preface

The General's Women has been a project in the making for over four years. While researching for my book, *Gaijin Shogun General Douglas MacArthur Stepfather of Postwar Japan*, I became intrigued with information about his private life, especially relationships with various women before he married Jean Faircloth. I had the pleasure of serving in the General's personal security force, known as the Honor Guard, in Tokyo, Japan, in 1951. It was near the time President Harry S Truman relieved the General of command, ending his military career.

I had known the General only as a remote iconic figure and had the highest respect for him as did others of his command. However, as I began to see him as a man subject to difficulties and failures in relationships with women, he became more real and endearing to me. Some have suggested that showing his shortcomings demeans his image. I truly do not believe that is the case. I trust that others who read this account will, as I have, develop a deeper understanding and admiration for the General.

My serious writing, which began after I retired from a business career, was directed toward non-fiction. However, I had a sense that *The General's Women* project would benefit from a woman's perspective. A local writer's group that I joined introduced me to Betty McElhatten, who joined me in this project as co-author. Betty is an experienced writer with a good sense of history. She not only provided the needed woman's perspective, but also reined me in if I ventured too far from historical facts.

This work has been created and developed in a manner that lends itself to direct use as a stage presentation. Permission for private or public presentation must be obtained from the authors (dvalley1@san.rr.com.) Director notes are available.

David J. Valley

Valley & McElhatten

Acknowledgements

We wish to express our appreciation to the General Douglas MacArthur Foundation for their support and permission to use photographs and the copyrighted letters and poems of Douglas MacArthur. Thanks are also extended to the William Clements Library, University of Michigan, for the material concerning Florence Adams.

Thanks to our family supporters and friends, especially Faith Frances Berlin who has worked closely with us editing and offering her advice and improvements to the presentation.

We also wish to acknowledge the literary license we have taken to make this work interesting to the audiences and readers we hope to reach. All interviews, including all dialogues, except quoted letters, phrases, and poems so indicated, are fictitious. However, the content they reveal about the General and his women is based on factual material previously published, or from the MacArthur Foundation archives and other reliable sources.

The Authors

Valley & McElhatten

Introduction

In these creative, fictional first-person interviews spanning almost 100 years, we introduce the man Douglas MacArthur, and the women in his life. Though a brilliant and world-renown military leader, General MacArthur's romantic relationships failed in one romance after another. It was not for lack of effort and application on his part. He wooed the fairer sex determinedly with grace, charm, and highly poetic words. As a romantic figure, he seemed idealistic at times, like a re-incarnation from centuries past, not fully in touch with the women he courted. Other times he was distant and dismissive and gave the impression of being a thoughtless Casanova.

Some say, because of his extremely close bond to his mother, MacArthur was unable to develop a satisfactory relationship with a woman for most of his life, except for a brief first-marriage. This may be true, for it was only after his mother's death when he was 57 years old, that he finally achieved a fulfilling and lasting love.

These interviews are in the style of a popular present-day TV journalist. With access to love letters and poems, and the gossip of the day, "Bobbe Waters" probes the principals to uncover titillating details of Douglas MacArthur's love life. The interviews ultimately reveal a personal side of MacArthur never before exposed. Whether MacArthur treated the objects of his affection callously, or if his behavior was within the bounds of acceptable courtship, is left for the reader to decide.

**C
A
S
T

O
F

C
H
A
R
A
C
T
E
R
S**

in order of appearance ...

ANNOUNCER - Off-stage speaker who sets each scene and provides background information.

BOBBE WATERS - Fictitious journalist and inter-viewer, a la today's TV journalists.

MRS. MARY MACARTHUR - Mother of Douglas, wife of General Arthur MacArthur, a strong-willed Southern lady of refinement.

DOUGLAS MACARTHUR - Famed 20th century military leader.

FLORENCE ADAMS - American student Douglas met on his first assignment in the Philippines.

LUCRETIA LEBOURGEOIS - Young New Orleans debutante enamored of Douglas.

FANNIBELLE STEWART - Urbane New York girl whom Douglas hoped to marry.

HERTA HEUSER - WWI German Red Cross nurse who cared for the disabled Douglas.

LOUISE BROOKS MACARTHUR - Wealthy socialite and divorcee whom Douglas married.

ISABEL ROSARIO COOPER - A young Eurasian beauty from the Philippines whom Douglas kept hidden away in a Washington hotel suite.

DREW PEARSON - Popular *Washington Merry-Go Round* columnist and journalist.

JEAN FAIRCLOTH MACARTHUR - Attractive and refined Southern lady; second wife of Douglas.

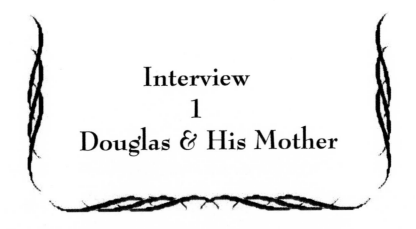

Interview
1
Douglas & His Mother

1903

A Suite in Craney's Hotel, just off the campus of
the United States Military Academy at West Point

The scene is a nondescript cluster of three chairs; the center seat for the interviewer, the others for guests. The re-enactment is created for a present-day audience who, like the reader, will witness the dialogue. House lights dim as an off-stage voice begins...

Announcer: Ladies and Gentlemen, you are about to participate in a unique historic adventure as the renowned journalist and intrepid interviewer, Bobbe Waters, transcends time and place to conduct first-person interviews with Douglas MacArthur, the ladies in his life, and others. Much is known of Douglas MacArthur's public life, but little of his personal life has ever been revealed, especially his romantic relationships.

Our first interview takes place over one-hundred years ago at Craney's Hotel, just off the campus of the United States Military Academy at West Point. The first guest is Mrs. Mary Pinkney MacArthur, mother of Douglas. She is an austere, stern-looking lady, about 50 years old. She appears older in her dark floor-length dress, upswept hair and fashionable black hat. This daughter of a wealthy Virginia merchant caught the attention of Captain Arthur MacArthur who was the most decorated soldier of the Civil War. They married and had three sons. The first, Arthur III, next Malcolm, who died at a young age, and then came Douglas to whom she gave first priority. Now, let us welcome Miss Bobbe Waters and her guest, Mrs. MacArthur!

Stage lights come up to bright showing the ladies seated.

Bobbe   Good evening, Mrs. MacArthur.

Mrs.
MacArthur   How do you do, Miss Waters. It's a pleasure to
             meet you.

Bobbe   The pleasure is mine. Thank you for consenting to
             this interview. Mrs. MacArthur, isn't it highly
             unusual for a cadet's mother to be in residence at
             Craney's Hotel, virtually on campus, during her
             son's years at West Point? Didn't this raise an
             eyebrow or two?

Mrs.
MacArthur   Perhaps, but let me give you a little background.
             Our family has moved about a great deal in the
             past. You may know my husband Arthur is a well
             known general and a career military man. He is
             now on extended service in the Philippines; our
             older son Arthur III is away in the Navy. We have
             never had what you would call a family home. I
             feel the need to be close by my dear Douglas. He
             needs the consistency of my presence in his young
             life and I covet his company.

Bobbe   .   Are there other mothers or parents who have
             established residences nearby?

Mrs.
MacArthur   *(Stand-offish)* I really wouldn't know.

Bobbe   Wasn't this living arrangement an embarrassment
             for your son?

Mrs.
MacArthur   Please understand we have an extremely close
             relationship. My primary concern is for Douglas's

well being and education. My efforts so far have been successful. Are you aware, Miss Waters, Douglas will graduate first in his class?

Bobbe   Yes, I am. I congratulate you and Douglas, but even so, wasn't your extreme proximity an embarrassment for your son?

Mrs.
MacArthur   Embarrassment? On the contrary, my influence steadies and guides him. I have developed a profound awareness of the sensitivity and strengths of my son; failure at any level that might cause him to falter on his path to glory is unacceptable. I am a constant support to him, and feel certain we are on the right course. It is my duty to do all in my power to prevent Douglas from stumbling into any foolish mistakes or despair.

Bobbe   Mrs. MacArthur, your loyalty and strong bond to your son is evident and quite admirable, but I'm not sure you answered my question.

Douglas MacArthur comes on the scene and takes the empty chair. At 23, he is a handsome man, tall and slim, with dark hair and eyes. Angular features give character to his still boyish face. He is dressed in ordinary cadet attire, a high-necked gray jacket with a bold black stripe down the center and gray trousers with black stripes. The West Point emblem on the small cadet cap, and oversized chevrons on the sleeves are the only adornment of his uniform.

Bobbe   Hello, Douglas. Perhaps I can get your view of a subject I have been discussing with your mother?

Douglas   Hello, Miss Waters. And thank you, sweet lady. I have been listening. I am ever grateful for your thoughtfulness and kindness to my dear mother.

Bobbe   You're welcome. Do your recollections and thoughts coincide with the statements she made?

Douglas   Yes, of course, for the most part. One's mother often has a clearer picture, especially of early events in her child's life. I may remember some things a tad differently, but never to the point of contradiction. Perhaps you would understand our close association better if I tell you how I managed to get into West Point.

Bobbe   Please go on.

Douglas   I tried for two years to get a congressional appointment, but despite my mother's and father's connections and persistence, I did not succeed. My mother then persuaded me to seek an appointment by way of competitive examination. For the better part of a year she supervised my studies and coached me. I owe my success to her and feel I can still benefit from her guidance and support.

Bobbe   I see you are a dutiful and respectful son, but I'd still like to ask you about your early days at the Academy. How was it when your fellow cadets, especially upperclassmen, learned your mother was at the Craney's Hotel?

Douglas   I believe it stirred a number of reactions. No doubt some resented it, perhaps wishing their own mothers could be nearby. Some labeled me a "mama's boy," and others didn't think much about it, I imagine.

Bobbe Did you have to put up with taunting over being labeled a "mama's boy?"

Douglas There was some of that, but I took it as a part of the hazing that is the lot of all first year cadets. Yes, I had my share.

Bobbe From what I've heard you had more than your share. Not only because of your mother's presence, but because your father is a famous general. Weren't they extra hard on you?

Douglas Oh, I don't know about that.

Bobbe Didn't the hazing get so out of hand you were called to a congressional inquiry about it?

Douglas Actually the inquiry was not directly related to me, but I was called to testify. Unfortunately, it put me in a delicate position.

Mrs.
MacArthur I'd like to add that I counseled him extensively on this matter, Miss Waters. Briefly stated, I told him he had to be honest, but careful not to disgrace the Academy.

Bobbe How did it go?

Douglas Quite well. I managed to answer the senators' questions without further incrimination of the Academy. In the end it proved to be a turning point for me. After it was over I became something of a campus hero and was even befriended by upperclassmen.

Mrs.
MacArthur   Yes. *(She says proudly)* And his friends took special delight in social visits to my suite for a respite. I greatly enjoyed their company and discussions. On occasion I served them snacks and a tot of wine.

Bobbe   I've heard you also entertained some of Douglas's lady friends. Is that true?

Mrs.
MacArthur   *(Affronted)* Well, I wouldn't call it entertainment.

Bobbe   Perhaps I should ask you, Douglas. I've heard tales about your romantic exploits. Rumors persist that from a young age you've had a great affinity for the female population.

Douglas   *(Laughs)* That's a rather, err.., a broad statement.

Bobbe   *(Chuckles)* I believe you set the record for most engagements during your senior year. Eight young ladies, is that correct?

Douglas   That's highly exaggerated.

Mrs.
MacArthur   *(Sternly, looking at Douglas)* But not entirely. I've had to sit down with several young women who mistakenly thought you were serious about a so-called proposal.

Bobbe

What did you say to them?

Mrs.
MacArthur

(Pompously) I simply told them they could not marry Douglas, because he was already married—to the Army.

Bobbe

And what did you think of your mother's dismissal of your lady friends?

Douglas

(With a smug look) Mother's always right.

Bobbe

(Smiling at Mrs. MacArthur) You're probably relieved that he will soon graduate.

Mrs.
MacArthur

(With resignation) I certainly am.

Bobbe

So what's next for you, Douglas?

Douglas

I'm off to the Philippines for my first assignment.

Bobbe

Are you happy with that?

Douglas

I'm absolutely thrilled!

Bobbe

Bon Voyage, Douglas. I hope to see you and your mother again.

End of interview

Interview
2
Douglas re Florence

1905

A New York City hotel suite

As the stage lights go up, the audience sees Bobbe seated in the center chair, waiting for her guest to arrive.

Announcer   Little is known about the romantic pursuits of Douglas from the time he left the military academy and went to the Philippines until he returned in late 1904. Miss Waters is about to interview Douglas and discuss an episode of his private life during that time.

Bobbe   Hello, Douglas. I understand you returned from the Philippines a few months ago, but this is the first chance I've had to welcome you back. Did you enjoy your assignment?

Douglas   Hello, Miss Waters. I'm happy to be home, thank you. As to my assignment, it was great. I did some engineering work on Leyte and got to see Luzon and other parts of the country.

Bobbe   I've heard you also made an interesting new acquaintance before you left Manila.

Douglas   *(He smiles broadly)* Now I wonder who that might be?

Bobbe   A Miss Florence Adams. Remember her?

Douglas   Of course. She's a lovely young lady. I met her shortly before I left and saw her a few times. It was nothing serious.

Bobbe   Oh, really? Perhaps there's another Douglas MacArthur?

Douglas   I don't understand. What are you talking about?

Bobbe   I'm just having a little fun. I'll say this though. I heard about your romantic pursuits at West Point, but I had no inkling of your literary skill. You do have a certain flair for writing passionate prose.

Douglas   You still have me at a disadvantage, Miss Waters, but I'm beginning to suspect Florence has been sharing my correspondence with you.

Bobbe   And then some. I've seen your letters, your shipboard diary and a portion of Florence's diary from the period when you were seeing one another.

Douglas   *(Eyebrows shoot up)* Her diary?

Bobbe   Oh, yes. Let me find my notes. Here we are. You were quite a dancer, in fact you first met Florence at a dance. The Pasay Hop. You also danced with her on three other occasions at Pasay, two more times at the Army & Navy Club, three occasions at the Dancing Club, two occasions at the 7th Infantry Hop, and two occasions at the 20th Infantry Hop. These dancing hops seemed to be popular venues for young men and women to meet.

Douglas   Yes, that's true, but my friends and I went stag and mingled with the young ladies there. It wasn't as if Florence and I were going together as a couple.

Bobbe   I understand that, Douglas. You are quite correct.
           But I can even tell you which number you were on
           her dance card. These were socials, but you also
           met separately on many occasions. Shall I enu-
           merate?

Douglas   *(Smiles smugly)* Yes, please do. This is quite
           interesting. I'm curious as to the <u>extent</u> of your
           information. Of course, I reserve the right to
           challenge any misstatement.

Bobbe   It seems your principal activities, when you and
           Florence were relatively alone, were those
           occasions when you went horseback riding—that
           was two times; carriage riding—seven times;
           dining together—ten times; and when you called
           at her home—five times. Does that sound about
           right to you?

Douglas   It seems a lot for the short time I knew her, but if
           she kept such detailed records, they are probably
           more accurate than my memory. Frankly, I'm
           more curious about other details.

Bobbe   Are you wondering if she may have written
           something intimate?

Douglas   Well—who could know what a young lady might
           write in her diary, whether truth or fantasy.

Bobbe   Relax, Douglas. Her diary chronicles your many
           meetings, but in very cryptic remarks. Nothing
           revealing—I'm sorry to say. What is more telling,

however, was written by <u>you</u>. I'd like to read the letter you wrote just before your ship docked in California.

"My Sweet Child: I wish I had the power to adequately express my thoughts of you and to you. They would be so exquisitely tender, so reverentially loving, that all other lovers reading would feel a pang that their love was such a starveling thing compared to mine.

"Do I hear you laugh, Sweetheart, that rippling infectious laugh, which always had its birth in your eyes but whose echo still rings in my heart? As always the mere thought of it makes me smile in sympathy, a smile which will end in a sob of loneliness and longing for you.

"It has been a thousand times worse for me than I thought it would be. I feel like a man who has been under the knife, but instead of losing a leg or an arm, my very soul seems to have been taken out.

"Unconsciously, I hear my lips framing the words wrung from Jesus Christ in his hours of agony, 'How long, O God, how long?'

"Do I sound wild, incoherent, extravagant? Perhaps, but bear with me. It is goodbye, Sweet Girl, for a few days, but remember that I am thinking of you always."

Bobbe	It seems to me that you go to extremes such as, "my very soul seems to have been taken out," or using the words of Jesus Christ at the time of his Agony in the Garden. Really Douglas—
Douglas	Why, Miss Waters, has life been so kind to you that you have never been separated from a loved one and had to suffer deep yearnings and emotions?
Bobbe	Oh, I have been separated from loved ones, but I must confess I have not experienced any such traumatic emotions. And just a moment, didn't you say to me at the outset that your relationship was not serious?
Douglas	I think what you are missing, Miss Waters, if I may offer the observation, is the time factor. I was absolutely sincere at the time I wrote that letter, but time changes one's feelings.
Bobbe	That's true enough, but in your case it seems to happen with great rapidity. It reminds me of that quip, "When I'm not near the one I love, I love the one I'm near." Is that you, Douglas?
Douglas	I don't believe I'm so frivolous, but as I said, "time changes one's feelings."

End of interview

Epilogue: Florence Adams's relationship with Lt. Douglas MacArthur covered a few months time span. Her diary entries never gave Douglas's name. She refered to "he," "him", or "we," in describing their activities. We know nothing of Miss Adams after Douglas sent a New Year's greeting to her in 1905.

Interview
3
Douglas & Lucretia

1907

New York City hotel suite

Bobbe Waters is seated center stage. The house lights dim as the stage lights brighten.

Announcer: We next hear about Douglas's romantic pursuits after Lucretia LeBourgeois appears on the scene in 1907. She is a rather self-assured young woman with a dramatic flair.

She enters stage left holding a packet of letters tied with purple ribbon. She takes the seat to Bobbe's left.

Bobbe   *(To audience)* It's been a few years since we have heard anything about Douglas MacArthur's romances. Recently, however, I found a young lady who was the object of Douglas's affection. She seems eager to talk about her experience. Here she is now.

Hello, Miss LeBourgeois, I'm pleased to meet you. Would you care to enlighten us, regarding Douglas MacArthur and that interesting handful of envelopes you are clutching?

Lucretia   *(Waving letters and sniffling slightly)* Actually, Miss Waters, this is all I have left of Douglas's declaration of love for me.

Bobbe   Oh? Tell me about it. When and where did you meet him?

Lucretia   It was in April, 1907, at Aunt Martha's home in Washington D.C. *(Lucretia rambles on)* You see, both of my parents died when I was quite young. Aunt Martha and Uncle Henry Wadsworth, well, anyway, they have always been most generous with their time and love for me and my siblings. They gave the most splendid parties for young people. It was at one such gathering that Douglas appeared.

Bobbe   What was your first impression of him?

Lucretia   Well, he did stand out in the crowd, being so tall and handsome in his uniform. Most dashing. His name was all over my dance card, although most times he preferred to sit on the veranda. He held my hand and recited poetry. I was totally enthralled by his charm.

Bobbe   Did he begin courting you immediately?

Lucretia   Well, yes, he did, except when he was on assignment in Pennsylvania. *(Lucretia pulls a letter from packet and waves it.)* I was thrilled to see his very first letter when it arrived within days of our meeting. He wrote it while staying at the Fort Pitt Hotel.

Bobbe   Would you be willing to share it with us?

Lucretia   Why yes, Ma'am. I'll just read it. It's not very long.

"Lucretia Dear Child: This is just a line to pass onto your sweet hand. It has been a ghastly long evening for me … my only consolation the knowledge that from the instant I left you, every minute that drops by brings me so much nearer.

"The wild spell has been with me again and all night long. I have been fighting it out with myself to keep from going to you like a thief in the night. Too late now, you must have been asleep there many hours—but I can bespeak you at least sweet dreams. Mine will be so, for I know they will carry me across the broad stretch of Washington town—and to thy side—sweet lady."

Bobbe   You must have made quite an impression on the young officer. Did you respond to his letter?

Lucretia I surely did. Then, just a few weeks later I was visiting with my brother, Joseph Charles, at his summer home in Pass Christian, Mississippi— that's near New Orleans, where everyone escapes the city to get away from the heat and yellow fever. *(Lucretia pulls second letter out and holds it up.)* This letter was delivered there . . . and Douglas expressed his love for me not once, but <u>three times</u> in the very first paragraph.

Bobbe   I'd love to hear that passage.

Lucretia I can just as well read the whole thing. It's not all that lengthy.

Bobbe   The first paragraph will do.

Lucretia "My Sweet Child:

There is little to write of from these gloomy barracks, save to tell you the old, old story—I love you. I love you—love you. How many countless millions in every land, in every age have used the same phrase. And yet, as I whisper it to you now, how poignant with meaning, how heavy with memories the words seem to be."

Bobbe   Douglas certainly doesn't waste any time in getting to the point.

Lucretia   *(Again waving packet)* Oh, I have more. His third letter reached me at my Aunt's house in Avon, New York on May 31st.

Bobbe   You obviously have read these letters many times and even memorized the dates. Do you always carry them as you travel about? And, who's your Aunt that lives in Avon?

Lucretia   I do visit around a lot with my family, but it's my same Aunt Martha who lives in Avon. It's her <u>summer</u> residence. They're only in Washington during the social season. As to remembering dates, well, you never forget when someone first tells you he loves you. I was totally smitten with Douglas. He captured my heart instantly and I believed he truly loved me. Then, when his letters abruptly ceased, he broke my heart and caused me no end of grief. *(She looks up)* Is that he?

Douglas enters stage right and sits on Bobbe's right. He glances at Lucretia and nods his head.

Bobbe   Hello, Douglas. You know this young lady I trust. She is quite enamored with you, or at least with your endearing correspondence. She's been sharing a few of your letters. Tell us, were her replies as expressive and captivating as yours?

Douglas   I really don't remember. We only exchanged a few messages over a limited period of time. It was merely a fleeting friendship between two recently-introduced young people.

Lucretia	Douglas, don't you dare treat me as if we were simply pen-pals!
Douglas	My dear Lucretia, you are a darling, but a most impressionable young lady. I'm afraid you have read far more into our relationship than was intended in my meager correspondence.
Lucretia	*(Sniffling into handkerchief)* But you did say you loved me, Douglas, and missed my sweet lips and soft hand. You said you felt a tenderness for me. You. . .captured my heart with your poetic zeal.
Douglas	My dear Lucretia. It was springtime. You and I know well what happens to a young man's fancy that time of year. Please consider that I was a lonely soldier at a remote post. Our relationship was nothing more than a pleasant, but passing, romantic exchange of a few letters over a short span of time.
Lucretia	Well, I certainly didn't see it that way! In my opinion, Miss Waters, Douglas takes advantage of innocent young women with his flowing sentiments, only to abandon them at a whim. *(Lucretia turns to Douglas)* Sir, you may be an officer, but a gentleman would not toy with a girl's affections. You ended our beautiful relationship leaving me totally distraught. I hope you're not writing more of your deceptive sentiments, arousing other unsuspecting young girl's hearts.
Bobbe	Now, now, Lucretia. No need to be so harsh. Perhaps you did misread his intentions. By the way, I can't help but notice a flashing diamond ring on your left hand. Is that a friendship token or something more significant?

Lucretia   *(Holds up hand to show ring)* This is a truly meaningful expression of deep and ever-abiding love. I'm engaged to be married in October to my beloved Robert Osborn Van Horn .

Lucretia rises, putting on airs of being offended, leaves the stage.

Bobbe   Well, Douglas, I'll bet you're relieved to hear of Lucretia's wedding plans. It seems you <u>did</u> lead her down the garden path.

Douglas   Not at all, Miss Waters. She obviously wasn't any more serious than I. You see how quickly she is getting over me, now soon to be married. Her relationship with Mr. Van Horn must have been long standing.

Bobbe   Even so, one would hope that witnessing her emotional reaction to your persuasive pen might dampen your profligate declarations of love to other . . . oh, let's say, passing fancies.

Douglas   Dampen my ardor? *(Douglas smiles)* I think not. You see, I perceive all women as wonderful, enticing creatures. There's no harm in enjoying and celebrating their charms. But even so, I don't want to marry everyone I meet.

Bobbe   Just keep that thought in mind when you write your next letter, Douglas.

Douglas   I'll try to take your advice to heart, Miss Waters, but it may be difficult. Goodbye.

End of interview

Epilogue: Lucretia LeBourgeois married Robert Van Horn in 1908. Robert rose to the rank of brigadier general in the U.S. Army. Lucretia studied painting with Diego Rivera in Mexico City; was a member of the San Antonio Art League, and became the mother of two daughters. After Robert's death in the 40's she moved to Palo Alto, California, where she died in 1971.

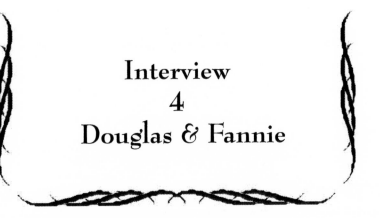

Interview
4
Douglas & Fannie

1908

New York City hotel suite

Bobbe Waters is seated alone, center stage, as the house lights come up. The announcer begins his introduction.

Announcer   A year ago, in 1908, Douglas reached a low point in his military career. His assignment was working on flood control projects for the Army Engineers in Wisconsin.

Out of boredom and frustration he feels indifferent to his duties, and is close to ending his budding military service. As an escape he becomes focused on his social life...especially toward a certain New York lady who has caught his fancy.

Ms. Fannibelle Stuart is a savvy young woman from New York's upper East Side. Here she is now.

Fannie enters—and sits.

Bobbe   How do you do, Miss Stuart? Your first name is Fannibelle?

Fannie   *(Smiling warmly)* Yes, quite a mouthful, isn't it? Please call me Fannie.

Bobbe   I shall. Fannie, let's talk about Douglas MacArthur. How did you come to know him?

Fannie   We met in Milwaukee. I was visiting relatives over the Christmas holiday. We were introduced at the Winter Carnival Ball.

Bobbe   He's a handsome young man, very striking in his military uniform. Were you immediately attracted to him?

Fannie   Oh, yes, along with a dozen or more of the local girls, but he took special notice of me.

Bobbe   Your attributes are obvious, but was there some <u>other</u> reason?

Fannie   Yes, I remember his exact words. He said, "Your sophistication is a refreshing change." I guess he was getting bored with those Dairy State girls.

Bobbe   Did he court you?

Fannie   I was only there for a few weeks, but we saw each other many times. And, would you believe it? On our second meeting he proposed!

Bobbe   Really. I gather you didn't accept.

Fannie   Heavens no! I liked Douglas, but I was hardly ready for marriage. There was too much fun to be had, and Daddy promised me a trip around the world.

Bobbe   So Douglas gave up on you?

Fannie   Oh, no. In between our visits there wasn't a day went by that I didn't receive a love letter in the mail.

Bobbe   A letter every day! Do you have any you could show me?

Fannie   Only a couple. I accidentally discarded most of them when I came back to New York. Here's one I kept.

Bobbe   Please read it.

Fannie   It's dated January, 1909. It's a poem called, *Why Not?*

       "Fair Gotham girl
       With life a whirl
       Of dance and fancy free,
       'Tis thee I love—All things above
       Why cans't thou not love me?"

Bobbe   Oh dear. Here we go again. It seems Douglas has trouble keeping his pencil in his pocket. Was this after you rejected his proposal?

Fannie   Yes. You see, I thought when I got back to New York that would be the end of it.

Bobbe   And it wasn't?

Fannie   Not hardly. There were letters with poems almost every day. I have a couple of the poems. *(She shows papers)* The one I received after I went to Paris was like a <u>book</u>, and so morbid and scary. I was relieved to be out of his reach. I stopped writing, and he soon gave it up, too.

Bobbe   You say his poem was scary?

Fannie   Maybe that's not the best word for it. Would you like me to read the shorter one?

Bobbe   Please.

Fannie   It's called, *The House of Dreams.*

The General's Women

"I live in a little house of dreams
In a land that cannot be—
The country of the fain desire,
That I shall never see—
Save with the waking eyes of dreams,
The land that cannot be.

"Why should I tell of my house of dreams?
You have been with me there
You know the walls of joy and pain
And you did not find them fair.
My little dusky house of dreams,
Dark with your hanging hair—

"You have kissed our little children's lips
And held them on your knee,
My little dream boy has your smile,
He is so dear to me—
His eyes are lit by the strange light
Not seen on land or sea—

"I close the door to my house of dreams
Lest the eyes of the world might see
What is far too pure for an earthly eye,
A dream love's ecstasy—
So I close the door to my house of dreams
In the land that cannot be."

Bobbe   I see what you mean. It is rather intense for a girl your age. You're about 20?

Fannie   I just had my 21st birthday. You know, Miss Waters, I've never dated an older man before, and if this is what it's like, I'll stick to the young ones.

Bobbe   Douglas is about 30, I believe. Is that what you'd call an older man?

Fannie It's not just his age. It's his seriousness. I'm not ready for that, especially after I received this lengthy poem in Paris.

Bobbe Tell me about the poem, Fannie.

Fannie Well, he began with a note saying he wanted to tell me what it would be like to be married to a soldier. He even said his being so candid would probably put me off, but he believed, in the "interest of fair play," he should be completely frank with me. Funny thing, I wasn't even thinking of marrying him, but after I read his 26-page poem, which he called a jingle, I was happy to be on the other side of the globe.

Bobbe What was the poem about?

Fannie It was a fantasy, I guess, about me being married to him. According to the poem we had children and he had to go off to war. It was very frightening and emotional. And then he comes back wounded, and it goes on and on. I'll read a little bit of it so you'll get the idea.

Bobbe Please do.

Fannie This is from the first part, supposedly quoting my words when I knew he had to go off to war. It goes:

"Our cause is so holy, so just, and so true—
Thank God! I can give a defender like you!
For home, and for children—for freedom—
for bread—For the house of our God,—
for the graves of our dead—
For leave to exist on the soil of our birth—
For everything manhood holds dearest on earth.

"When these are the things we fight for—dare I.
Hold back my dear treasure, with plaint or with sigh?
My cheek would blush crimson—
my spirit be galled if you were not there when the muster was called!
I grudge you not, Douglas—die, rather than yield,
And like the old heroes, come home on your shield!"

Bobbe I'm impressed. Interesting poetry, but very intense and, I might add, morose. I can understand why you wouldn't be ready to marry into a situation like that. Well, Fannie, this has certainly been a fascinating look at the courting behavior of Douglas MacArthur. Thank you sharing it with us. Goodbye, dear.

Fannie exits the stage while Bobbe remains seated. Immediately thereafter Douglas enters and takes the seat to Bobbe's right.

Bobbe Douglas, it's good to see you again. I've just had a most interesting discussion with Fannie Stuart; I'm trying to keep abreast of your love life. Apparently you were quite taken with her.

Douglas Oh? Why would you think that?

Bobbe Please, Douglas, your romantic missives leave trails as blatant as footprints in the snow.

Douglas I can't imagine what you are talking about.

Bobbe Well, how about that 26-page "jingle" you wrote. Fannie felt it painted a scary picture. I didn't see the whole piece, but she read part of it to me.

35

Douglas   That was personal. *(He looks perplexed and hesitates a moment)* I thought a woman would want to know what kind of life she would be facing if she married an Army man.

Bobbe   *(Shaking her head)* Douglas, you are an interesting and attractive man, but you have a knack for going to extremes in your relationships.

Douglas   I don't know what you mean.

Bobbe   Oh, I think you do. You move far too swiftly with the women you're attracted to. Some, like Lucretia, fall madly in love with you, only to be casually tossed aside. Others, like Fannie, are put off by your dramatic seriousness and your quick proposal. Aren't you aware of the consequences when you unleash all that romantic ardor?

Douglas   Now who's taking this too seriously, Miss Waters? Romantic words and imaginings are all part of the game of courtship for young people.

Bobbe   Well, I won't even give you a pass on the _young people_ part, after all you must be nearing 30. Most men at your age are married and have families.

Douglas   I guess I just haven't met that special person yet. If I could only find someone as attractive and intelligent as you, my search would be over.

Bobbe   *(Laughs)* Don't try to butter me up, Douglas. I'll be keeping a sharp eye on you.

Douglas   I'm flattered by your interest. Goodbye for now.

End of interview

Epilogue: Fannibelle Stuart later lived in New Orleans with her husband Casewell P. Ellis, who was in the cotton business. They were close friends with the parents of Lucretia LeBourgeois's sister-in-law. Fannibelle was related to the Dorothy Gray Cosmetic Company and it was also reported that her family was somehow connected to the murdered Stanford White, who in 1906 was found dead at New York Madison Square Garden's Rooftop Theatre. White was America's leading architect, designer and arbiter of taste.

Valley & McElhatten

Interview
5
Douglas & Herta

1920

A New York City hotel suite

Announcer   It's said that it takes a war to make a great soldier. Certainly that was the case for Douglas MacArthur, who prior to WWI was a minor officer without particular distinction. On the battlefield, however, his courage and leadership—even when disabled—resulted in rapid promotion to the rank of brigadier general. After a period of convalescence in Germany, MacArthur returned as one of America's most decorated heroes. We learn, however, even when physically disabled, Douglas lost little of his romantic verve, as Bobbe Waters reveals.

Bobbe   *(To audience)* I read in the *New York Times* that the International Red Cross is meeting in New York to discuss aid for Europe. The name Herta Heuser, one of their representatives, caught my eye. Could this be the woman whose letters from Douglas MacArthur found their way to me? This would be almost too good to be true. I asked Herta to meet with me.

Bobbe looks nervously at her watch, wondering if her guest is going to show up. A woman enters, looking around with uncertainty.

Bobbe   Ah, over here! *(Bobbe waves)* Welcome to America, Fraulein Heuser.

Bobbe waits for Herta to be seated.

Herta   Guten Morgan, Miss Waters.

Bobbe   Hello. There's so much I'm eager to talk to you about, Herta. First, I understand that your family's home in Germany at Sinzig on the Rhine, was used as General MacArthur's command post during the closing days of World War One.

Herta   Ya, dass is correct. I, as well as other members of my family, continued to reside there in order to provide services for the General and his staff.

Bobbe   I see. And what were your specific duties during that time?

Herta   Fortunately, I am a Red Cross Nurse. I vas able to give expert medical care to General MacArthur. He vas recovering from poison gas and diphtheria.

Bobbe   Herta, I've heard that you corresponded with your patient after he returned to the United States. Wouldn't that have been considered a form of fraternizing, which was prohibited for Germans in occupied Allied territory at that time?

Herta   *(She furrows her brow and hesitates)* Nein. Even though the war did not end for another ten months or so, we were definitely not enemies. Ach! This fraternization policy makes no sense.

Bobbe produces a bundle of papers.

Bobbe   Perhaps not. In any case, would you explain to us what the General was referring to in his first letter to you dated May 16, 1919 . . . and I quote: "Keep well that which you have of mine. It stays with you as a contented prisoner and longs to help you in this terrible hour. God be with you till we meet again. Douglas."

Herta   *(Looking confused)* Why, *(She pauses)* it refers to nothing more than a strong bond of ...friendship.

Bobbe   Ahhh . . . but the next letter boldly expresses the general's affection for you. *(She shows a particular letter)* Clearly this was written after the censorship of letters had been stopped. He wrote, "I love you with all my heart and soul." He talks about seeing you again and is eager for you to come visit him in the United States.

Herta   Was is los? I am appalled at your invasive questioning. I am also mystified and most curious as to how letters addressed to me, personally, found their way to <u>your</u> prying eyes. Please, may we discuss what I was led to believe was my real purpose in meeting with you . . . as a representative of the International Red Cross.

Bobbe   I'm sorry if this has been uncomfortable for you, Herta, but we Americans have an insatiable interest in famous people and you and the General do seem to have a <u>romantic</u> history.

Herta   Nein! My relationship with General MacArthur was strictly professional in nature. It was not uncommon for a disabled soldier to think himself in love with the nurse who administered to his needs.

Bobbe   That's true, but then why did you write to <u>Mrs. MacArthur</u> trying to locate Douglas?

Herta   I don't know where you get such information!

Bobbe   But you don't deny it, do you? Also, it seems obvious that Mrs. MacArthur must have spoken to Douglas about your relationship. That's when he wrote to you that it wouldn't work out.

Herta   Ridiculous! You are making this up!

Bobbe   Let me read this to you, Herta. You decide if I'm making it up. This letter, dated September 12, 1919, was addressed, to you:
"My Dear Herta: Mother has asked me to write you saying she received a letter from you asking my whereabouts. *(Bobbe pauses and looks at Herta to verify the point)* I fear my letters have either been miscarried, censored, or stolen. The difficulties of our respective positions are so great as to be impossible to overcome. I have realized this lately and believe we had best face it frankly. My Army Command makes me a servant of the Republic and I feel that I am no longer a free agent. My respect and admiration for you will be with me always, and there will ever be a niche in my heart marked with your name. But together, we can only look backwards, not forward. May God be with you until we meet in another and kinder world." It is signed, Douglas.

Herta   *(Flustered)* I demand you destroy those letters and insist you cease to even mention them again. Auf Wiedersehen, Miss Waters.

Herta quickly rises, glares at Bobbe, turns and briskly marches off.

Bobbe   *(To audience)* I guess I've been properly admonished by the annoyed Fraulein Heuser. Obviously, she wasn't about to admit to anything. Perhaps Douglas will share some information about his relationship with the German nurse. Will he deny any intimacy, or any promises he might have made? This might be interesting!

The lights momentarily dim, then rise again. Shortly thereafter Douglas enters and sits next to Bobbe.

Bobbe   Douglas. It's always a pleasure to see you. How have you been?

Douglas   Very well thank you, Miss Waters. And you?

Bobbe   First, let's dispense with the Miss Waters business, please call me Bobbe. And I am very well, thank you. I read in the newspaper that you will soon be the Superintendent of West Point. How do you feel about that?

Douglas   It's the best assignment I can imagine, and I'm honored, as this post usually goes to a more experienced Army man.

Bobbe   I know of your war record in Europe; I'd say you've earned the position. But I want to ask you about events as the war was winding down. I've recently spoken with someone you met in Germany. I'd like to talk about your time in the Rhineland, when you were recuperating.

Douglas   Whom have you been talking with?

Bobbe   I'll tell you in a minute, but first tell me how you were doing after you took command of the 84th Brigade in early December, 1918.

Douglas   Hmm. It seems you have the right points of reference. You must have been talking to an Army man. Correct?

Bobbe   Later, Douglas. But just give me a briefing, I think that's a word you use.

Douglas   Let me think a moment. Yes, it was about the first of December. I had led the brigade on a 155 mile march from Luxembourg into Germany, the area referred to as the Rhineland. We were in reserve, as part of the occupation forces, to give us time to mend. I was still suffering from the effects of poison gas and had a mild case of diphtheria. About 25 miles south of Bonn we came upon the village of Sinzig. It had that story-book, medieval look. I commandeered a magnificent place, right on the Rhine. It became my home and headquarters until I was well enough to return to America.

Bobbe   Were you bed-ridden at the time?

Douglas   No, I was ambulatory, but still weak and needing to rest frequently. I had good care though. Fortunately, one of the castle's residents was a nurse. She looked after me.

Bobbe   Do you remember her name?

Douglas   Of course. It was Herta. *(A quick smile, he pauses)* Yes, Herta Heuser.

Bobbe   *(She quickly changes the subject)* Douglas, tell me how things were going with the occupation at that time?

Douglas   For the most part fairly well. We didn't have any die-hard Germans in our sector. The situation was generally peaceful. I had a string of visitors those days, too. Some were quite notable, like the Prince of Wales. He and I had a grand time for a few days, talking about all sorts of things. I remember the Prince was very concerned that the

Germans might rise up again. I said, "We beat the Germans this time, and we can do it again."

Bobbe   Isn't it true that you didn't entirely agree with the occupation policy which banned fraternization between Americans and Germans?

Douglas   Off the record, I certainly did not. As my father taught me long ago, don't ever issue an order that you know will not be obeyed. And, let's face it, nature is a most powerful driving force. When young people are attracted …well, you know. Furthermore, what better way is there to bring about peaceful relationships? Our diplomats should take a lesson.

Bobbe   *(Laughs)* That's an amusing thought! Well, now that I understand your philosophy on the subject, I can see where you and Herta Heuser might have had an intimate relationship.

Douglas   *(Stern and adamantly)* I did not say that! *(He looks at Bobbe quizzically)* What are you doing? Trying to out-fox me? I should have known. What do you <u>think</u> you know about me and Herta?

Bobbe   Douglas, you know it's my business to have sources. One of them somehow got hold of letters you wrote to Herta. From those I've seen, it seems to me you had more than just a patient-nurse relationship. Just how intimate were you?

Douglas   I'm going to deny any intimacy, of course. A gentleman does not talk of such things, not that there was anything to talk about.

Bobbe   Then let me just ask you this: Would you be interested in continuing your relationship with Herta, such as it was, say, if she came to America?

Douglas   *(Shaking his head)* I have fond memories of her, but there's no basis for a continuing relationship.

Bobbe   *(Sighs as if disappointed)* Such being the case then, I shall drop the subject. I thank you for the time, General, and I wish you great success at West Point.

Douglas   Thank you, Bobbe. Despite your zealous over-reaching intrusion into my personal affairs—bad choice of words—I mean my personal life, I still consider you a friend, and I appreciate your good wishes. Goodbye.

Douglas walks off the stage.

Bobbe   *(To audience)* At one point I had high hopes of playing cupid. I thought I might bring Douglas and Herta together for a renewal of their romance, but obviously there's no interest on his part.

End of interview

Epilogue: The letters written by Douglas MacArthur to Herta Heuser date from 1919 to 1920. They were discovered in recent times by the sons of a U.S. Army WWII soldier attached to the 518th Military Police Battalion that served throughout Europe, and, at one time, in the area of Sinzig Germany. Copies of the letters were sent to the General MacArthur Memorial Foundation in 2000.

Interview
6
Douglas & His Mother,

1921

A New York City hotel suite

Announcer   After a few month's duty in Washington, America's popular hero was given one of the most prestigious commands in the Army: Superintendent of the U.S. Military Academy at West Point. Though consumed with his plan to revise the school's out-of-date curriculum, the 40 year-old bachelor found time to give expression to his ever-present romantic urgings.

As the stage lights come up we see Bobbe seated in the center chair. Mrs. MacArthur enters, stage left, and sits on Bobbe's left.

Bobbe   Years ago we discussed Douglas's romances, Mrs. MacArthur. *(Who looks skeptical)* Now, there's something about Douglas and a German girl.

Mrs.
MacArthur   *(With disinterest)* Oh, that. *(Pause)* It was merely a situation where Douglas was trying to show his gratitude to a young woman who helped with his recovery after the war.

Bobbe   But the letters I saw surely indicated a romantic interest. Do you deny that?

Mrs.
MacArthur   Please. It's not worth going into, dear. *(She waves her gloves to dismiss the subject)* Let's just say Douglas was indebted to the woman; that's all there was to it.

Bobbe   I'm not so sure... but in any case there is a romantic interest in Douglas's life now. I've just met Louise Brooks.

Mrs. MacArthur	Oh yes. *(Haughtily)* <u>The</u> Mrs. Brooks, socialite, Lady about Town. She and Douglas have been seeing each other.
Bobbe	I understand Douglas has already proposed.
Mrs. MacArthur	*(Quickly)* I don't know about that. Of course, it wouldn't be the first time he's mentioned marriage to one of his fancies. I doubt it's serious.

Douglas enters stage right, nods politely to his Mother.

Bobbe	Well, let's ask Douglas. Nice to see you again. Please be seated. *(He sits to Bobbe's right)* I've been talking to your mother about Louise Brooks.
Douglas	I'm not surprised you're still on my tail, *(quickly corrects)* I mean trail.
Bobbe	*(Laughs)* Oh, Douglas, you're so transparent!
Douglas	And you, Miss Waters, are so speculative. I thought reporters were supposed to stick to the facts.
Bobbe	You know better than that. If we stick to the facts our stories would be too boring. But that admission aside, are you not courting Louise Brooks? Have you not proposed?
Douglas	*(He casts a glance at his mother)* Ah...I'm, ah... *(He sits back in his seat resigned to admit the truth—pauses)* We're not ready to announce it publicly, but I have asked her to marry me.

Mrs. MacArthur rises from her chair and casts a hard look at Douglas. He waves to settle her down.

Douglas   *(Pleading)* Mother, please be seated. *(She sits)*

Mrs.
MacArthur   Douglas, don't tell me you are really going to marry that woman. Why, she's been involved with <u>so many</u> other men. She's a divorcee, with children yet!

Douglas   Mother! Please don't speak of Louise that way. She's really a fine lady; very sophisticated, and intelligent. We're in love.

Mrs.
MacArthur   *(With distain)* In love! Oh please, Douglas! I know it's just physical. You poor boy. *(She sighs)* Excuse me, Miss Waters, this is just too overwhelming for me. *(She stands and walks toward the exit stage left, stops and says,)* I'll speak to you later, Douglas!

Looking very concerned, Bobbe turns to Douglas.

Bobbe   I didn't know your mother was unaware of your engagement. I'm sorry my statement led to her becoming so upset.

Douglas   Don't worry. She'll get over it once she gets to know my fiancée. She'll soon discover that Louise is a wonderful person.

Bobbe   Well, I hope so, for the sake of all of you. *(She pauses)* Douglas, there's something I'm curious about. Isn't your mother living with you in the Superintendent's residence at West Point? *(He nods a yes)* What are your plans after you marry?

Douglas   *(Frowning)* What do you mean?

Bobbe   Well, Louise will be living with you then and... *(Bobbe pauses, trying to draw a response)*

Douglas   *(Annoyed)* <u>And</u> mother, too!

Bobbe   Are you and Louise clear about that? Does she realize the three of you will share the house? Have you discussed it with her?

Douglas   *(Pauses)* Not in so many words, but I'm sure she understands I must look after my mother.

Bobbe   Pardon me for saying so, but looking after your mother, and sharing your home with her during your honeymoon period are two very different things.

Douglas   Your imagination is running wild again, Miss Waters. You do have a penchant for looking for trouble in the most tranquil places. *(Offended)* I believe it's time to end this interview.

Douglas begins to exit stage right, pauses when Bobbe speaks

Bobbe   Please excuse me if I've offended you.

Douglas turns to walk away.

Bobbe   Douglas... Please!

Douglas   *(With a forced smile)* Okay, Miss Waters *(With an ominous look)* —This time.

End of interview

Valley & McElhatten

Interview
7
Louise

1922

A New York City hotel suite

Announcer   It's been a month since the MacArthur-Brooks wedding. This report comes from the *Palm Beach Sun*'s society editor. I quote: "Douglas and Louise were married at a fashionable ceremony on Valentine's Day, February 14, 1922, performed at the Stotesbury's Spanish-style Palm Beach villa *El Mirasol.* The ceremony was scheduled for 4:30 p.m. Apparently, when Douglas arrived at 4:00 o'clock, Louise was not yet dressed in her apricot chiffon wedding gown and diamond necklace. He proceeded to lecture her on punctuality and she reportedly pouted. The guest list included 200 names, yet only one was a representative of the MacArthur family. MacArthur's mother 'Pinky' refused to attend; her absence did not go unnoticed. After the honeymoon, the couple moved into the superintendent's house at West Point; Pinky moved back to Washington's Wardman Park Hotel." End of Quotation.

Bobbe is seated center stage. Louise walks in and sits next to her.

Bobbe   *(To audience)* Let's talk to the newlywed in person. Hello, Louise.

Louise   Hi, Bobbe. Nice to see you.

Bobbe   And you too! Thanks again for inviting me to your lovely wedding. It was a grand affair. So many interesting people. But I was disappointed not to see Douglas's Mother, or meet any of his family members.

Louise   I know. Aside from a friend of Douglas's, there were no guests from his side. I did all I could to extend invitations. His mother sent regrets saying she was ill. Sick of me, I believe.

Bobbe   Now, Louise, don't be too harsh on her. You know she isn't that well. You just have to give her a chance to know you better. Enough of that. *(Said joyfully)* Tell me, how goes the honeymoon?

Louise   *(She giggles)* Everything's wonderful with me and Douglas!

Bobbe   Great! Now tell me: has Mrs. MacArthur moved back to West Point?

Louise   Oh, no. There was some discussion, but that would never do. *(She laughs)*

Bobbe   Why not? *(Bobbe smiles in anticipation of a juicy disclosure)*

Louise   Oh, I shouldn't. *(She lowers her eyes shyly)*

Bobbe   C'mon, just between us girls.

Louise   *(Laughs again loudly)* Well, the way Douglas hoots and hollers and cavorts in bed. Honestly, I think it would give the old girl a heart attack.

Bobbe   *(She laughs and leans close to Louise—soto voce)* Is he such a passionate lover?

Louise   He's an animal! *(Laughs)* But that's not the whole story. I've known animals before, but never one with the heart of a poet. Let me read one of his romantic notes. I have dozens of them. Ahem. "My adorable: I have been drunk with the intoxication of you all day. The caress of your eyes, the tenderness of your lips, the sparkle of your wit! The gleam of your smile makes my pulse shiver, the touch of your hand my head swirl, the warmth of your mouth suffocates my gasping senses and leaves me stunned and shaken with the glory and wonder of you as I enter Paradise."

Bobbe — Oh, my goodness. *(Bobbe fans herself)* Let's get back on track. *(She looks intently at Louise)* My intuition tells me something is bothering you.

Louise — You are so astute, Bobbe. Would you believe Mad Jack has cut short Douglas's West Point assignment and is sending us to the Philippines?

Bobbe — Mad Jack? Are you referring to General John Pershing?

Louise — Yes. I am. We were close friends once, but *(She casts a knowing look at Bobbe)*, that was in Europe after the war. It was just a brief fling. Jack already had his eye on a Belgium beauty, but then he introduced me to his aide, Col. John Quekemeyer. Quek is a handsome man, but he certainly lacked his boss's, shall we say…vigor. It just didn't work out, despite Jack's encouragement. So when Douglas and I got together, Jack was really put out. He warned me not to marry; said I'd regret it. Now he's sending us across the globe to some god-forsaken islands.

Bobbe — Well, that's quite a story. How is Douglas taking it?

Louise — Right in stride! Wouldn't you know? Typical Army business, he says.

Bobbe — You don't agree?

Louise	Look, Bobbe, I don't know much about the Army, but I know Jack. He never liked Douglas MacArthur. I heard that in Europe, long before I knew the young general. Jack thought Douglas was too big for his britches with all his wartime heroics and awards. And then we married despite his admonition. This is definitely Jack's retribution.
Bobbe	I'm surprised petty things like that go on in the Army.
Louise	Hah! It's no different in that regard than our civilian society.
Bobbe	I see your point. Well, tell me, will you be leaving soon?
Louise	Yes, and I'm just beside myself. There's so much to think about. I was debating whether or not to leave my children in school here, but Douglas insists on bringing them with us. It really surprises me that he takes such an interest. I'm truly grateful that he's being such a wonderful stepfather to them. And then I've got to think about my social calendar—I had so many exciting things planned for the upcoming season—drat! What will I do? I'll be so alone over there. Will you come to visit me? Oh, Bobbe, I promise to make it worth your while. I'll even buy the steamship tickets! What do you say?
Bobbe	Are you serious? *(Louise nods noticeably)* That's certainly a generous offer. I'll give it some thought. I'll write to you. In fact, if you find you don't have much to do, drop me a note from time to time and I'll keep you abreast of what's happening around the city.

Louise   I'll be waiting to hear from you. Please don't forget me.

Louise exits stage left, stops, turns to Bobbe, waving with a forlorn look.

Bobbe   *(To audience)* I certainly won't forget her. I suspect Louise Brooks MacArthur will be good copy for a long time to come.

End of interview

Interview
8
Douglas & Louise

1923

The lobby of the Manila Hotel, Manila,
Philippines

Announcer   Douglas has accepted his transfer to the
               Philippines in good grace and seriously pursues
               his military duties. Louise tries to cope with her
               new life in what she considers an unfriendly
               environment. Now, thanks to a sudden
               unexpected assignment, Bobbe Waters has an
               opportunity to meet Louise again.

As the stage lights brighten, we see Bobbe seated, center stage.

Bobbe   *(To audience)* Surprise, surprise! Here I am at the
               historic Manila Hotel. I called Louise MacArthur
               last night after I arrived. She was excited to learn
               I was here and will be meeting me soon. Ah, here
               she is now. Hello, Louise. You look lovely.

Louise   Well, thank you, dear, and you are looking *trés
               chic*. Is that dress the latest fashion?

Bobbe   Of course. I bought it just before I left. *(Pause)*
               You and I had quite a telephone conversation last
               night. I didn't realize I knew so much New York
               gossip until you dragged it out of me.

Louise   Are you kidding? You could put Walter Winchell
               out of business if you weren't so dedicated to this
               interview business. I'm so happy you came.

Bobbe   As I told you it was just a fluke. The Travel Editor
               suddenly took sick and someone had to cover the
               Asian Ports of Call story. I'll be leaving tomorrow
               for Hong Kong.

Louise   So soon? I was hoping you'd be here for a while.
               I was thinking of having a big party for you; let
               you meet the locals.

Bobbe   That's very thoughtful, but no such luck. I'd better stick to my agenda for the little time I have. I'd like to see Douglas, too, before I leave.

Louise   He's due back today. I'll have him call you if he returns in time.

Bobbe   So tell me. How is life in Manila?

Louise   In a word boring. Don't tell Douglas, but I hate it here. I don't know how long I can stand it, Bobbe. The weather, the social life, the monotony. It's dreadfully dull!

Bobbe   I can see what you mean about the weather. Is it always this bad?

Louise   No. It's often worse. It's the kind of weather that would drive you to Newport if you were back East in the summer—sadly there's no Newport to run to here. But that's not the worst of it. I'm just so lonely.

Bobbe   But you have Douglas and the children. And, what about the children? How are they doing?

Louise   Oh, they are having a great time. They have many interesting friends from the international school. Douglas absolutely spoils them when he's around, and, of course, they each have their amahs to cater to their needs. I don't know what I'll do with them when we go home. They're fine; it's me that's not.

Bobbe   I don't understand, Louise. What's wrong?

Louise   Oh, where do I begin? I guess I'm just not suited for Army life. I knew it would be different, but I wasn't prepared for this. Douglas is gone much of the time doing maneuvers or some silly thing. He's been away almost a month now mapping some desolate part of this island. I've resorted to reading his old love letters as a comfort. *(She withdraws a stack from her handbag)* These were written when we were courting.

Bobbe   Why don't you read one?

Louise   Alright. Here's one written from the Academy; written before we were married.

"You adorable piece of loveliness: You are to my thoughts as food to life, as sweet seasoned showers are to parched ground. When you are near I am full with feasting on your sight—when you are far I am clean starved for a look. No delight I feel save what is from you. Thou are the world's first adornment. How beautiful you are! Like unto a summer's day. But thou art more lovely. Rough winds do shake the darling buds of June and spoil its facing. But thy eternal loveliness shall not fade as long as men can breath or eyes can see. I wish I might have the wit to tell thee how I love—but alas, I cannot. Thou must learn to read what silent love hath failed to pen. Forgive me if I do rave, I do but love thee." *(She abruptly crumples the paper)* No woman is content with a piece of paper! He should understand that.

Bobbe   I'm not sure of your meaning. He should understand what?

Louise   *(She looks left and right)* He should understand that a woman needs adult company.

Bobbe   Hmm. Have you found some interesting companions here?

Louise   It's been a challenge, even for someone of my wiles. You can forget about the native population. Douglas has many friends among the government and business leaders here, and I must admit their wives are quite beautiful, but we have nothing in common. And then, most of the men of the international set are small-time company heads, or boring bureaucrats.

Bobbe   So what remaining segment holds some attraction? Don't shake your head, Louise. I can sense someone is sparking your interest.

Louise   Well, there <u>are</u> one or two from the diplomatic corp of countries I won't mention that…shall I say, I have found interesting.

Bobbe   Do you mean intimately?

Louise   No, I'm not saying that. But I wouldn't mind if Douglas thought I was interested. It would serve him right.

Bobbe   What do you mean, "it would serve him right." Has he been unfaithful to you?

Louise   Heavens no. He's so traditional. What's the word the jazz musicians use; *square*? That's him and he's deeply committed to our marriage.

Bobbe   Then why? Why would it "serve him right?"

Louise   Oh! *(She gestures wildly with her hand)* It's his <u>mother</u>. He's more attached to her than me.

Bobbe   But she's not here.

Louise   No, but when she was sick a while ago, we had to rush back to America to be at her side.

Bobbe   Well, Louise, I wouldn't worry. She's an old lady and she'll not be around forever. But tell me, what lies ahead for the future? Will Douglas be transferred back to the States any time soon?

Louise   Unfortunately, I don't think it will be soon enough. Honestly, I don't know how long I can put up with being alone like this, despite my occasional dalliances.

Bobbe   I quite understand, and I wish you the best, Louise. Shall we continue our exchange of occasional letters?

Louise   Oh, please do. I so look forward to them. *Bon Voyage,* my dear!

Louise leaves the stage with Bobbe. The stage lights go dark, then come up to bright.

Announcer   It is later that same day when Bobbe returns to the lobby of the Manila Hotel to meet Douglas. The General is dressed in his casual uniform with an open-neck shirt. His only adornments are the single stars on his collar. It is apparent the hotel staff accords the General their attention and respect.

Douglas spots Bobbe and waves to her. They meet in the center of the lobby and shake hands.

Douglas   Hello, Miss Waters!

Bobbe   Hello, Douglas. It's a pleasure to see you again!

Douglas   And you, too, Miss Waters. *(Douglas leads her to a secluded table in the Champagne Room)* We'll have more privacy here. Did you have a good passage?

Bobbe   Quite good, except I was seasick the first couple
             of days out of San Francisco. After that it was all
             smooth sailing. So, how are things in the
             Philippines, and how is married life?

Douglas   As to the Philippines, all is well in these beautiful,
             peaceful islands. And, as to married life, I
             couldn't be happier. I have always longed for a
             home and hearth, a loving wife and children.
             Thanks to Louise I have everything my heart
             desires. It's marvelous!

Bobbe   I'm happy to hear that, Douglas. As one who has
             witnessed the romantic interludes of your past, I
             often wondered if you would ever settle down to
             married life and find contentment.?

Douglas   Oh, I have wanted to for years. Now I have every
             intention of enjoying it to the fullest.

Bobbe   Tell me about your assignment. Do you think you
             will stay here for a long time?

Douglas   Well, you can never be certain about things like
             that in the Army. Like at West Point; I expected
             to be there another year and the next thing I knew,
             I was off to the Philippines.

Bobbe   I imagine Louise shared her thoughts with you
             about that. As you know, I visited her earlier
             today. She told me she felt sending you to Manila
             was a vindictive move on the part of General John
             Pershing. How do you feel about that?

Douglas   I was disappointed to leave West Point before I
             had fully accomplished what I set out to do. I'll

admit to that. But as far as questioning the motives of my superiors, that is simply not done.

Bobbe   At least not in public.

Douglas   No comment.

Bobbe   I can see you make the best of your Army life and you look like a happy man. But do you think life in the Philippines is as satisfying for Louise and the children?

Douglas   No doubt Louise misses the social life she enjoyed in America, but now she's an Army wife and stays the course. The children, who are wonderful, by the way, seem to be enjoying life here immensely.

Bobbe   I suppose I shouldn't be talking out of school. *(She almost chokes on that)* But are you sure Louise is all that content for you to continue pursuing your Army career?

Douglas   We've talked about the possibility of my taking a position in business, but as I've explained, I must uphold my commitment to the military in the tradition of my family. She understands.

Bobbe   I am sure she does, but even so I imagine she would like to return to America before too long.

Douglas   No, I wouldn't say so. Louise has really gotten into the swim of things here. I don't know how long my assignment might be—another year or more—but she'll be content. I'm sure.

Bobbe   Really? *(With raised eyebrows)* Well, on another subject, how is your mother? I understand she was quite ill for a spell and you made an emergency trip back to the States.

Douglas   Yes, it was a close call. Mother's recovering now, but she <u>is</u> getting along in years and her health is fragile. She's the one who is anxious for us to be back. Speaking of being back, I've been away on a long assignment and I've much to catch up with. I must say goodbye for now.

Bobbe   Of course. Goodbye, Douglas. My best wishes to you and your family. I shall look forward to meeting you again when you return to America. Goodbye.

End of interview

Interview
9
Louise

1929

A New York City townhouse

Announcer   After three years in the Philippines, Douglas was transferred back to Washington. He, Louise and the children moved into a sumptuous estate, a home which was part of Louise's inheritance. However, their domestic tranquility gradually deteriorated. They separated and Louise took up residence in New York. We listen in as Bobbe and Louise meet in the lobby of a townhouse on Central Park South.

Louise had been standing alone. Bobbe walks in to join her.

Louise   Hello, Bobby. Welcome to Treymore Arms.

Bobbe   Good to see you again, Louise. I can't believe it was nearly five years ago that we met in Manila.

Louise   Yes, dear girl, it's been a long campaign. *(She laughs)* For all I've been through, I should be the one getting the medals. Let's go upstairs to my place.

Lights dim on stage, then brighten again. They are now seated.

Bobbe   This is a gorgeous view! I could live like this.

Louise   *(With resignation)* You wouldn't want my life, dear.

Bobbe   Perhaps not all of it. *(Pause)* Now, what were you saying in the lobby? You ought to be the one getting the medals? For what? Would it be for escapades in the Philippines?

Louise   No. It would be for all I've had to put up with being married to Douglas.

Bobbe   Can I assume then that all is not well with you two?

Louise   (*Archly*) Don't patronize me, Bobbe. Although we haven't met here in New York the past couple years, I'm certain, with your ear to the ground and all your spies, you are quite aware that my marriage is nominal to say the least.

Bobbe   Ouch. You caught me. I should know better than to mince words with you, Louise. In fact, I'll share the latest I picked up off the grapevine. I have it on good authority that your attorney is drawing up divorce papers. Will you confirm that?

Louise   My God, you do have good sources. I was in my lawyer's office only yesterday. The answer is yes, and good riddance!

Bobbe   Just for the record, what are the grounds for divorce?

Louise   You'll love this! I could have chosen any of a dozen different causes, but the one that especially amused me was economic hardship. *(She laughs)* I'm claiming Douglas cannot support me in the style I'm accustomed to!

Bobbe   Are you serious? You? One of the wealthiest women in America, claiming economic hardship? What in the world will Douglas say?

Louise   Oh, he just wants to get it over with, so he'll agree to anything as long as I don't impugn his precious image. I consented to keep it quiet. That is, except for sharing it with my friends.

Bobbe   It is amusing, Louise, but wait... I need to backup a little. Exactly what happened to your marriage since I saw you in Manila? I knew you were depressed, but I didn't know you were actually considering a divorce at that time. Were you?

Louise   I certainly was, but Douglas was so adamant about making our marriage work, and he was so persuasive, I didn't pursue it. He promised me the life I was accustomed to when we returned to America.

Bobbe   That must have pleased you.

Louise   It did, and I thought it would all work out when he was transferred to a post in Baltimore, near the old family home I inherited. It's a gorgeous country estate, fit for a king. Why not for King MacArthur? *(Laughs)* We even changed the name to *Rainbow Hill* after his precious Rainbow Division, of WWI. I must admit I was caught up in the excitement as I made renovations and planned for the social season. We had numerous dinner parties, balls, fox hunts, and we attended all the local society events. I was having a grand time, and... I was a good girl.

Bobbe   You mean...?

Louise   You know what I mean. I was the dutiful wife. But something changed with Douglas. He had always been the one with the stiff upper lip; stay the course, always upbeat, that sort of thing. But after about a year in Baltimore it was as if someone let the air out of him.

Bobbe   What do you think happened to him?

Louise   I don't know, but in one of our rare, frank exchanges, Douglas admitted he felt emasculated.

Can you imagine! He said his military position had no substance, and our social life was meaningless to him. That hurt me, because the social life _is_ my life. Douglas never understood that. There was just no pleasing the man. I told him he needed to go fight a war, and he agreed! After that I moved here to my home in the city.

Bobbe   Are you lonely? What's it been like for you?

Louise   It's good. It's as if we're not married. I do as I damn please, and I guess he does the same.

Bobbe   Do you think he has a _par'amour_?

Louise   I doubt it. He's such a traditionalist. A few months ago he called, flattering me, trying to make a go of our marriage, he said. He may have been sincere, but I think he's only concerned about his public image.

Bobbe   Do you two have any relationship at all now?

Louise   Actually no. Just business details; things like that.

Bobbe   No torrid love letters?

Louise   Heavens no, that was over years ago. But I should add he always inquires about the children and he is sincere about that. Funny, he was a good father, but as a husband, bah...who needs him.

Bobbe   When was the last time you saw Douglas?

Louise   _(Thoughtfully)_ That would be... more than a year ago, just before he left for Europe. You know he was President of the American Olympic Committee. _(Bobbe nods yes)_   Of course, he did a good job. It was in all the papers. Now he's back in the Philippines; for how long I don't know and I don't care.

Bobbe   It looks like this chapter of your life has just about ended, Louise. What's in store next?

Louise   It may sound frivolous, but at this point in my life all I want is fun and parties, interesting people, social life, night life. You know.

Bobbe   Not like you do. *(She smiles)* Anyone particularly interesting you can tell me about?

Louise   I guess I can. There <u>is</u> a certain Hollywood actor I've been seeing a lot. He's a man who really knows how to party and have a good time, but I won't tell you his name.

Bobbe   Well, Louise, I wish the best for you in the future. Let's keep in touch.

Louise   As always Bobbe. Well, toodle-oo.

End of interview

Epilogue: Louise Cromwell Brooks MacArthur's marriage to Douglas lasted seven years. Louise then pursued her romance with the Hollywood actor, Lionel Atwell, and eventually married him—only to find he was much too much of a debaucher to live with, even with her sated lifestyle. Her third marriage also ended in divorce. In time Louise declined physically and mentally and disappeared from the social scene.

Interview
10
Isabel

1934

Lobby of The Wentworth Hotel,
Washington, D.C.

Announcer   In 1930, while on assignment in the Philippines, General MacArthur was awarded the Army's highest post, Chief of Staff, and reassigned to Washington, D.C. However, shortly before he left he was so bewitched by a certain young lady, he could not bear to leave her behind. The woman you are about to meet is Isabel Rosario Cooper, a stunningly beautiful Eurasian girl whose father was a Scotsman and mother a Filipino. Isabel's behavior suggests a maturity far beyond her years and tends to conceal her naivety. She has been MacArthur's secret lover now for four years.

Bobbe is seated as Isabel enters stage left and sits at Bobbe's left.

Bobbe   My! You are a breathtakingly attractive young woman, Miss Cooper. I can certainly understand the General's overwhelming interest in you. Where did you meet?

Isabel   At Manila's Olympia Stadium. I used to go there to see the fights. One night I noticed two foreigners in military uniform. A tall, handsome man with a chest full of bright ribbons kept looking at me. I gave him the look, too.

Bobbe   Were you introduced that night?

Isabel   Yes. The General sent the other soldier to me with a note. I returned one right back. I invited him to watch me perform in my vaudeville show.

Bobbe   And after that you started going out together?

Isabel   Sort of. He came to see me a lot. I even invented a special drink for him. I called it "Douglas."

He loved it. It was made with crushed mangoes,
Spanish brandy, and ice.

Bobbe   I didn't know Douglas was much of a drinker.

Isabel   He's not, but he liked everything I gave him. I can
tell you that!

Bobbe   Wow! Weren't you terribly young to be...
entertaining a man who was considerably older
than you? Serving him drinks, and ah...

Isabel   I'm not sure he knew my age exactly. I earned my
living as a dancer, and you know, entertainers
wear lots of make-up. It's hard to tell their age.

Bobbe   How long were you two friends before General
MacArthur was reassigned to Washington, D.C.?

Isabel   Friends? Oh, we were much more than "friends"
during those four months in Manila. It was
because of me that Douglas called it the happiest
time in his whole life.

Bobbe   When he left the Philippines for his new post,
weren't you afraid you might never see him again?

Isabel   Oh, no! *(She laughs)* We made big plans to always
be together. He told me he loved me. He even left
a ticket for me to take a ship and follow him as
soon as he was settled. He wrote to me every day;
sometimes twice a day. He called me his "Darling
One," and "Baby Girl."

Bobbe   Just how old were you when all this took place?

Isabel   Almost 17, and very grown up for my age. In my

country, that is old enough to marry and have children.

Bobbe Didn't you find it strange the General didn't take you with him?

Isabel Dougie told me it was against military rules for us to be on the same ship. He said we'd keep a little secret because he was so famous. All I know is that he wrote saying, my "deep lips and soft body taunted him and left him sweating with lust." I know what that means! He swore he'd "simply die" if I didn't come to Washington. Those were his exact words.

Bobbe Really? That's pretty steamy stuff. Ah, the General never ceases to amaze me with his romantic escapades. Such reckless behavior. Didn't your parents try to keep you in Manila?

Isabel My parents? No. I've been on my own for a long time. I got on that big ship alone. I arrived at Pier Number 9 in Jersey City on a cold December day in 1930, all alone. I'll never forget.

Bobbe And the General was on the dock to meet you?

Isabel You silly? Of course not. A big important man like Douglas sends a car and driver.

Bobbe Well, of course. I stand corrected. When was it you saw him?

Isabel The next night. He had a swell apartment all set up for me in Georgetown…all kinds of wonderful presents. It was the best Christmas I ever had. There was a fur coat he'd bought for me in Shanghai, a jade and diamond ring, and many pretty little things for me to wear. He was very glad to see me, I tell you!

Bobbe   That's quite an impressive list. The General seems to be a very generous man. Was the diamond meant as an engagement ring?

Isabel   Oh, no. Dougie didn't say anything about getting married. You know, I have girl friends in the Philippines who have rich and powerful men for boyfriends. They taught me you never say about marriage to such a man.

Bobbe   Probably good advice. Did the General spend a lot of time with you, once you arrived in Washington?

Isabel   Not so much. Many times he would telephone, "Daddy can't make it tonight." He'd say there was a special meeting he couldn't miss ... or that he had to do something... for his mother. A lot of times his mama needed him.

Bobbe   Did you have friends? What did you do with all that time on your hands?

Isabel   No friends then, and I hardly ever went out. I really got bored . . . sometimes mad. Dougie said we had to keep our love a secret. I don't know why. After all, he wasn't a married man!

Bobbe   Sounds like you were his captive love partner.

Isabel   Well, I guess I was, and sometimes I got tired of...the whole darn thing. When Douglas went to Europe, he signed his letters and postcards "Globetrotter." Boy! That made me mad and feel terrible. Here I was like a bird locked in a cage. I told him when he came home, next time he went traveling I was going to take off, too!

Bobbe   How did he respond to that ultimatum? *(Isabel gives Bobbe a questioning look)* What I mean is, that threat.

Isabel   Good, in a way. *(Smiles broadly)* He moved me to a big suite at the fancy Chastelon Hotel in Washington. That's when he decided to give me an allowance and a chauffer-driven car. Oh, and a whole new collection of lacy lingerie. That was really nice. Dougie promised he would spend more time with me, too, since I'd be closer to his office.

Bobbe   So, did you get out and about a bit more then? Was the General able to find time for you to be together?

Isabel   *(Disappointed)* Not really. And I was getting plenty mad. All the time I get last minute phone calls…with him so sorry sounding. *(Said mockingly)* "Dimples, Daddy has to meet with some very important people and I just can't come over tonight." Hah! Just only when he has hots in his pants!

Bobbe   Ahem! *(Pause)* Did you ever meet Douglas in a restaurant for lunch or dinner?

Isabel   Never! His mama must be some special kind of lady because he has his meals with her most of the time. I never met her. Dougie said she was "too delicate" to entertain me in their home. What do you think?

Bobbe   I think it's understandable. Mrs. Mac Arthur was always the number one priority in the General's life. So, Isabel, why did you continue to put up with that life style? Didn't you want to go out and do things with people your own age?

Isabel   Sure. But I didn't always put up with that. Like in Autumn of '32 when Doug went back to Europe for a few weeks. Just like I tell him before, I take off, too. I had a wonderful time in Havana. Boy!—He got so mad at me!

Bobbe   But then you returned to the same old pattern. Why?

Isabel   What do you mean pattern? You mean like I do before? *(Bobbie nods)* Well, Dougie, he begged me. He promised he'd change, spend more time with me. But the only thing <u>really</u> change, he spends more money on me. Hah! That's not so bad. I have a nice place, no rent. I didn't have to get up early, no going to work. Sure, it was boring, but not so bad.

Bobbe   But you had to be totally at his beck and call, didn't you? It's hard to imagine someone, with your beauty and youth, content with such a bizarre arrangement.

Isabel   Well, it wasn't always like that. Starting in '33, I did go out more on my own. I wasn't just staying around the hotel, waiting for him to show up. I went to a school and met lots of nice young people.

Bobbe   I've heard you had a special interest in a certain young law student. Did the General find out?

Isabel   *(Giggles)* Not right away. He thought we were just friends, but when he found out I was going out to nightclubs and had met a man from the State Department, wow! He really got mad. We had a big fight.

Bobbe   Tell me.   What did he say?

Isabel   *(Pouting)* He said I'm no good for him—no more! He gave me money and a steamer ticket. He told me, "Go back to the Philippines."

Bobbe   You'd been doing what he wanted for a long time, but this time you didn't obey the General's orders.

Isabel   Right!   After four years suddenly it was over. Okay, I accept, no more Dougie, but I'm not going back to Philippines. I cashed my ticket and found a cheap place to stay. It was good, but around September of 1934, I ran out of money. What could I do? I didn't know; I had to ask Dougie for more.

Bobbe   And how did the General respond to your request?

Isabel   He sent a mean note telling me I should ask my father or brother. He even sent Help Wanted ads clipped from the *Washington Times*. Like I should go get myself a job as somebody's maid! He signed it from "The Humane Society."

Bobbe   *(Trying not to smile)* That's a unique way to terminate a relationship. *(Then serious)* Four years, and you had nothing to show for it.

Isabel   *(She lights up again)* Oh, yes, I did! I had his mushy love letters, and I got paid plenty for them.

Bobbe   What do you mean? Black mail? Did you sell them to him?

Isabel   Oh, no. I met Mr. Drew Pearson, the newspaper man who writes *Washington Merry-Go-Round.* You know him? He accused Dougie of something and the General sued him, so Mr. Pearson wanted something he could use against Douglas, you see. And it wasn't just me. His ex-wife, Louise, told Pearson many bad things about him, too. I couldn't believe some of the things she said. Like Douglas was no good in bed. She was crazy.

Bobbe   This is all quite interesting, but wait a minute. I know about that lawsuit, however I didn't know you were involved.

Isabel   I wasn't until Mr. Pearson found me. He said he looked all over Washington for me. I showed him the letters, telegrams, and all those pretty postcards Dougie sent to me. You know, I was still very angry about the way he treated me. Pearson asked if I would go to court and I said sure. I could tell everything about our love affair.

Bobbe   But you didn't have to go, did you? I believe the lawsuit was settled out of court.

Isabel   Yes, and I was so happy. Actually, I was afraid to go to court. I think maybe they'd send me back to the Philippines. Anyway, all I had to do was give Pearson's lawyer that stack of letters and cards and I got $15,000! But I had to promise to keep quiet and never ask the General for money again. Oh-oh, am I saying too much? Well, I better not say anymore. It's been nice talking to you, lady. Bye-bye.

Isabel, looking very satisfied with herself, exits stage left.

End of interview

Epilogue: After Isabel's four year affair with General MacArthur ended, she married the law student, but soon divorced him and moved to Hollywood. Some reports say she had an interlude in Ohio where she tried her hand at the beauty business. Whatever the case, Isabel did not succeed in her attempt to break into the movies and become famous. She had numerous low-paying jobs in Los Angeles until 1960 when she tragically ended her short, unhappy life at the age of 47.

Interview
11
Drew Pearson

1934

**Crystal Dining Room at the Willard Hotel,
Washington, D.C.**

Announcer   Douglas MacArthur, now Chief of Staff, U.S. Army, attracted a lot of public attention and also some harsh criticism, especially from one member of the press, Mr. Drew Pearson. Criticism of the General in Pearson's newspaper column was deemed by MacArthur as slanderous and precipitated a high-dollar figure civil lawsuit. Bobbe has arranged a meeting with Mr. Pearson and is waiting in the Crystal Dining Room of the Willard Hotel.

Bobbe is seated alone at the table. She looks at her watch then looks around the spacious dining room.

Bobbe   *(To audience)* I'm expecting to meet the famed writer, columnist, and man-about-Washington, Mr. Drew Pearson. Ah, there he is! The distinctive, nattily attired gentleman with the trademark mustache. Hello, Drew. It's nice of you to see me on such short notice.

Drew   I'm always happy to accommodate a fellow member of the press. What brings you to Washington, Bobbe?

Bobbe   I'm intrigued with what you have been writing about Douglas MacArthur and your recent run-ins with him?

Drew   Oh, that. *(With disappointment)*

Bobbe   Just, "Oh that," from the voluble columnist about one of his most popular targets? I'm surprised.

Drew   All that is water over the dam. I must say you've caught me at a bad time.

Bobbe   Hey! It's not like you to pull in your horns. Does it have something to do with Douglas suing you for an ungodly sum?

Drew   Forget it, Bobbe. That's all behind us now. Our lawyers worked things out. I'm not at liberty to discuss the details.

Bobbe   Okay. Well, then, let's just back up a bit to before you got into litigation. You seemed to have a visceral dislike for Douglas MacArthur. Why is that?

Drew   I wouldn't exactly characterize it like that, but to me he does represent the epitome of the arrogance and the power of the military in our country.

Bobbe   Don't you believe we need a strong military to defend us?

Drew   Of course we do, in a time of war, but we're not at war. I believe it's their constant building of armaments and beating the drums that can foment a war. It doesn't seem long ago that we fought the "War to end all wars," but not according to our military.

Bobbe   This subject is not my strong suit, Drew, but it seems to me we need a strong military as a deterrent to discourage would-be dictators from springing up.

Drew   You're right, Bobbe—it's not your subject. That argument by the way, which is fostered by our military, is patently specious.

Bobbe   Alright, I'll stick to what I'm here for. What else can you tell me about MacArthur?

Drew
: If you really want some interesting tidbits, you ought to talk to Louise Brooks. Do you know her?

Bobbe
: Yes, I do. What does she have to say?

Drew
: Where should I start? She's saying the most scandalous and demeaning things. Problem is, I don't know if you can believe her. She told me all sorts of things, but when my lawyer asked if she would testify in court, she backed off like a scared rabbit.

Bobbe
: My, that doesn't sound like the Louise I know.

Drew
: She's probably changed a lot. She's really gone down hill since her failed marriage to that Hollywood actor. She's a mess. She's lost her beauty and appeal. She's gotten fat, and I think she overdoes the drinking, too.

Bobbe
: How sad. I've known Louise for years as a charming woman, full of life. I am sorry to hear of her decline.

Drew
: Yes, it's a shame. And you can chalk her up as another MacArthur casualty.

Bobbe
: Oh, Drew, I don't think that's fair. Louise just wasn't suited to be the wife of a military man. I'm surprised their marriage lasted as long as it did. What was it, about seven years?

Drew
: Around that. And you're right on that score. I can't imagine anyone being married to that pompous windbag so long!

Bobbe
: I do believe you're biased.

Drew
: I'll not deny that, but I'd better keep silent now before I wind up wasting my time with lawyers again and back in court. *(continued on page 91)*

1893 - Douglas MacArthur at age 13
(Photo: General MacArthur Memorial Foundation)

Douglas, about 16 years old, when a cadet at the West
Texas Military Academy
(Photo: General MacArthur Memorial Foundation)

1900 - Mrs. Mary Pinkney (Pinky) MacArthur with her son
Douglas at the U.S. Military Academy, West Point
(Photo: U.S. Military Academy Archives)

Lucretia LeBourgeois, circa 1904
(Photo courtesy of Julien LeBourgeois)

Mrs. Mary (Pinky) MacArthur with a photo of
Douglas when he was in Europe during WWI
(Photo: General MacArthur Memorial Foundation)

Brigadier General Douglas MacArthur during WWI. This photograph may have been taken at his headquarters on the Rhine at Sinzig, Germany.
(Photo: General MacArthur Memorial Foundation)

Brig. Gen. Douglas MacArthur, when Superintendent
of the U.S. Military Academy at West Point
(U.S. Army Photo)

West Point,1920 - Brig. Gen. Douglas MacArthur with the Duke of Windsor, who later became king of England and abdicated the throne for his lover Mrs. Wallace Simpson. It is interesting that both men experienced intense romantic relationships.

(Photo: Brown Brothers)

General John J. "Mad Jack" Pershing, 1918. As Army Chief of Staff, he allegedly cut short MacArthur's West Point assignment and sent him and his new wife Louise off to the Philippines.

(Photo: National Archives)

This picture of Louise and Douglas (right) with two of the General's aides was taken in Baguio in 1923. They were apparently recreating at this resort area outside Manila. Their attire may be described as the "natty" casual of the upper crust. Note the hat on Douglas's lap, known as a "straw boater skimmer."

(Photo: General MacArthur Memorial Foundation)

Douglas and Louise aboard the transport *Cambrai* headed back to America after three years in the Philippines. They were tough years for Louise, but for Douglas an Army assignment that suited him.

(Photo: General MacArthur Memorial Foundation)

Newspaper journalist and columnist, Drew Pearson, waged a scurrilous print campaign against Army Chief of Staff Gen. Douglas MacArthur, who sued for libel. The suit was settled when Pearson discovered MacArthur's secret lover and threatened to damage the General's public image.
(Photo: J. Wayne Higgs)

Manila, July 4th, 1936. President Manuel Quezon welcomes Gen. MacArthur to the Philippines after his retirement as U.S. Army Chief of Staff. The following month MacArthur was named Field Marshall of the Philippines. These were significant times for Douglas—he had met Jean Faircloth on the trip to the Philippines and began courting her; meanwhile his ailing mother, who had accompanied him to Manila passed away.

(Photo: credit unknown)

Build Me a Son
By Douglas MacArthur

Build me a son, O Lord,
who will be strong enough to know when he is weak,
and brave enough to face himself when he is afraid;
one who will be proud and unbending in honest defeat,
and humble and gentle in victory.

Build me a son whose wishbone will not be
where his backbone should be;
a son who will know Thee- and that
to know himself is the foundation stone of knowledge.

Lead him, I pray, not in the path of ease and comfort,
but under the stress and spur of difficulties and challenge.
Here, let him learn to stand up in the storm;
here, let him team compassion for those who fall.

Build me a son whose heart will be clear, whose goals will be high;
a son who will master himself before he seeks to master other men;
one who will learn to laugh, yet never forget how to weep;
one who will reach into the future, yet never forget the past.

And after all these things are his,
add, I pray, enough of a sense of humor,
so that he may always be serious,
yet never take himself too seriously.

Give him humility, so that he may always remember
the simplicity of true greatness,
the open mind of true wisdom,
the meekness of true strength.

Then I, his father, will dare to whisper,
"I have not lived in vain."

Douglas and Jean Faircloth were married in April, 1937 in New York. They immediately returned to the Philippines. A year later they had a son, Arthur IV. The family enjoyed three happy years in Manila until the Japanese invaded December, 1941. On Christmas Eve, MacArthur moved his family and headquarters to the Malinta Tunnel on the Island of Corregidor until their departure March 11, 1942

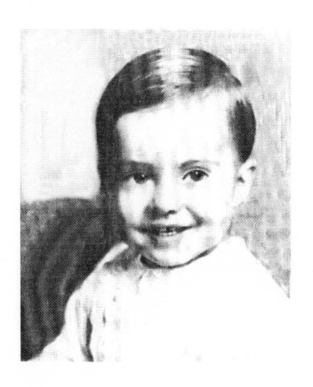

Arthur IV at a young age
In Manila, Philippines
(Photo: General MacArthur Memorial Foundation)

Australia, March, 1944 - Jean & Douglas - The Allied Forces were on the offensive. Two years earlier the General had been ordered by President Roosevelt to leave the Philippines. A few days later when he met the the Press in Australia, he issued his famous promise, "I shall return."
(Photo: U.S. Army)

October 20, 1944, Red Beach, Tacloban on the Island of Leyte. General MacArthur fulfills his promise as the liberation of the Philippines begins. Within minutes after this photo was taken, he was speaking to Filipinos by radio broadcast saying, "People of the Philippines, I have returned."

(Photo: General MacArthur Memorial Foundation)

After Japan's surrender, September 2, 1945, the Occupation of Japan commenced under Supreme Commander Allied Powers, General Douglas MacArthur. In 1946, the two five-star generals, MacArthur & Eisenhower, were reunited in in Tokyo, Japan. Eisenhower had served as MacArthur's aide for several years during the 1920s and '30s in the Philippines.

(U.S. Army photo)

Jean Faircloth MacArthur, Douglas,
and aide Laurence E. Bunker - center,
Tokyo, Japan about 1947
(U.S. Army Photo)

April, 1951, General Douglas MacArthur and family return to America and are greeted by record-breaking crowds. This photo is from a ticker tape parade in New York City.
(Photo: General MacArthur Memorial Foundation)

The MacArthur Family
Summer, 1951 in Brewster, New York
(Photo: General MacArthur Memorial Foundation)

MacArthur family support at the Waldorf-Astoria Hotel,
New York City, 1951. Ah Cheu - household,
Colonel Laurence E. Bunker - aide, and
Mrs. Phyllis Gibbons - Arthur's tutor.
(Photo compliments of Kiwamu Tsuchida)

Jean Faircloth MacArthur showing a favorite
picture of "her General"
Waldorf-Astoria Hotel, New York City
August, 1995
(Photo: General MacArthur Memorial Foundation)

General Douglas MacArthur Memorial, Norfolk, Virginia.
Final resting place of Douglas & Jean Faircloth MacArthur
(Photo: General MacArthur Memorial Foundation)

Bobbe   Thank you for your time, Drew. Goodbye.

End of interview

Epilogue: It was said that Drew Pearson's only regret about settling the suit with MacArthur was the loss of a favorite target for his anti-military theme. MacArthur paid dearly: $16,000 of Pearson's legal fees and a similar sum in a financial settlement to his former lover. When Fleet Admiral William Leahy learned of the General's capitulation and settlement with Pearson, he said, "MacArthur could have won the suit. He was a bachelor at the time. You know why he didn't fight it? It was that old woman he lived with at Ft. Myers. He didn't want his mother to learn about the Eurasian girl." To the General, preserving his mother's shining image of him was worth every dime of the more than $30,000 he paid; a huge sum of money in 1934.

The "Washington-Merry-Go-Round" column was syndicated to over 600 newspapers and had an estimated 60 million readers. Drew published ten books as well as a newsletter. With his controversial news gathering and muckraking reporting style he was involved in 50 libel cases, losing only one. Pearson remained an active contributor to broadcasting until his death in 1969.

Valley & McElhatten

Interview
12
Douglas

1934

The Plaza Hotel, New York City

Announcer   When Bobbe called Douglas with a casual inquiry about his present situation, she was surprised to learn he had been deliberately avoiding her. The General was concerned about the implications and content of their previous interviews. To assure him he had not been unfairly treated, she agreed to send transcripts for his review. They are meeting now to discuss his findings.

As the lights go up Douglas enters stage right and sits next to Bobbe.

Bobbe   Hello, Douglas. I hope you're feeling a little more kindly disposed to me. I was disturbed to hear you say this might be our last interview. I thought we were on good terms. Now that you have read all the transcripts, is something still bothering you?

Douglas   Yes, there is, Miss Waters. I've gone over all of them and frankly, the impression I'm left with is not a favorable one.

Bobbe   Whatever do you mean, Douglas?

Douglas   Although not stated in explicit terms, you have consistently characterized my innocent romances in a way that left the impression I'm some sort of villainous Lothario, or womanizer.

Bobbe   I think you're exaggerating, Douglas.

Douglas   No, I don't believe I am. You imply indirectly that I'm an abuser of women, or an aberrant man, or suggest I'm a lust driven animal. None of that is true. Is it a personal vendetta? Or are you one of those women who secretly harbor great animosity toward men and enjoy demeaning them?

Bobbe   Not at all! How could you take my remarks so seriously? It's true that I deal in titillating information, but I never meant to denigrate you. Who was it that said, "I'll accept any publicity, good or bad, just spell my name right?"

Douglas Perhaps it was a politician, but as for me, I hope I'm making it clear that I don't want or need any adverse publicity.

Bobbe   I honestly don't agree that it is. Believe me, Douglas.

Douglas I guess that's for others to decide, but let me set the record straight. While it is true that I have strong physical urges, I believe they are imbued by my Maker. It's a natural part of masculinity. Growing up I saw the stallion on the range, how he selected and frolicked with his filly, the intensity of their coupling, and yes, the tenderness afterwards. I believe we do a disservice to animals when we say a person acted as one. Most animals have a greater respect for one another than many humans.

Bobbe   Hold the reins, Douglas. I think you protest too loudly.

Douglas I don't believe I do. Please let me finish. It is important for you to understand that I have <u>never</u> forced myself on a woman. Every woman I have ever been intimate with was, at the time, the sincere object of my love. In my opinion, having a physical relationship is simply an expression of love, as are the words I put on paper. Others may judge my actions as … indiscreet, but who has the right to judge the depth or quality of the affection between a man and a woman?

Bobbe   Well, certainly not me. Perhaps you are right to chide me. Believe me, Douglas, I do respect you, but you know you are great copy. I also admit that I must pander to the public's interest. That's my job. That said, I believe both of us have benefited from our dialogues over the years.

Douglas   I'm not so sure. I think you've had the advantage at my expense.

Bobbe   Actually, Douglas, I'd put it the other way around. You've had your fun and never paid the tab.

Douglas   Oh. You've made your point, Miss Waters; hmm, a well-placed barb. *(He chuckles)* But even though you wound me, I confess, I do admire a clever, combative woman.

Bobbe   And I admire a resourceful Romeo, or is it that we are just mellowing with age?

Douglas   I may be mellowing, Miss Waters, but I still kick like an Army mule!

Bobbe   I won't touch that line, Douglas. So, is it 'til we meet again?

Douglas   I suppose so. *Au Revoir!*

Bobbe   Goodbye, General. I thank you for your frank disclosure and I do respect your honesty.

End of Interview

Interview
13
Douglas & Jean

1937

Lobby of the Waldorf Astoria

Announcer   Several years have passed since the last reported romance of Douglas. He concluded his term as U.S. Army Chief of Staff and is now a military adviser to the Philippines. The General, in his mid-fifties now, surprised many when he announced his marriage to a refined southern lady, Miss Jean Faircloth.

The lights come up, showing Bobbe waving to someone approaching her.

Bobbe   Jean MacArthur, it's a pleasure to meet you. I'm especially pleased you would take time to see me during your honeymoon. Shall we sit over here?

They are both seated.

Jean   The pleasure is mine. Douglas will be down soon, but he warned me, in the meantime, not to let you get too personal. Whatever did he mean?

Bobbe   I think I know, but I shall tread lightly. I'd like to know more about the woman who married the great General, and how you met. It doesn't need to get especially personal.

Jean   I'm sure you can tell from my speech that I'm from the South—Murfreesboro, Tennessee, actually. There's not much to say about my background. I've been engaged in charitable works and in my leisure time I like to travel. That's how I happened to meet Douglas. It was last year; I was sailing out of San Francisco to the Orient on the *U.S.S. President Hoover* when we met. The Captain was having a dinner party for the Mayor of Boston, Mr. Curley. We were both invited, and introduced.

Bobbe   What were your first impressions? Did he sweep
         you off your feet?

Jean   You might say that he did. I was most proud to be
         introduced to him. I knew what an important man
         he was, a great American hero, a legend. When he
         spoke to me… well, I just can't tell you how
         thrilled I was. But that night I didn't think he
         especially noticed me. However, the next morning
         a note was delivered to my stateroom, asking for
         the pleasure of my company on the quarterdeck
         for afternoon tea. I was so flustered it took me
         nearly two hours to decide what to wear.

Bobbe   Was it just the two of you?

Jean   Oh, no. His mother was there and another
         gentleman, a military man I believe, but he wasn't
         in uniform. The General's mother was ailing and
         seemed very frail. He treated her with such loving
         respect. When he introduced me he said, "Mother,
         it gives me the greatest pleasure to introduce a
         lovely lady from the South, Miss Jean Faircloth."
         Why you know, she took my hand and asked me
         to sit close to her. Though she was not well, I
         could tell from the intensity of her eyes that she
         was a very special person. She asked me many
         things about my family, our history, about my
         past. It was like an interview, though I didn't
         mind, as she was so engaging. After a while she
         turned to Douglas, who wasn't privy to our
         conversation, and said, "Too bad you didn't meet
         this young lady 30 years ago; she'd have been a
         perfect wife."

Bobbe   My goodness. You must have made quite an impression on Douglas's mother. What was his reaction?

Jean   Why he just grinned from ear to ear and said, "I told you so, Mother."

Bobbe   I'll bet that thrilled you. Did you spend a lot of time with Mrs. MacArthur after that?

Jean   Very little, actually. I wanted to, she was so fascinating to listen to, but her health was poor. She stayed in her stateroom most of the time.

Bobbe   But you did see a lot of Douglas?

Jean   Every day we walked the promenade. I was so fascinated by his stories. I loved the way he addressed me as he spoke, as if I were the most important person in the world. At the evening dinner parties we were in the same company and occasionally danced.

Bobbe   How did Douglas feel about sharing you with the other young men aboard?

Jean   Well, I love to dance and since he seldom ventured onto the floor, I often danced with other men. When I noticed he was watching, I did tease him a bit. You know, just a little flirting with my partner. I was truly fond of the General, but I couldn't imagine we had any future together, so I was having a little fun.

Bobbe   But what happened? I understand you decided not to continue your Asian tour and remained in Manila. What changed your mind?

Jean   Well, I had received an invitation to President Quezon's Inauguration while I was aboard, and I also have friends who live in Manila. They wanted me to stay with them... so it wasn't really that I changed my mind.

Bobbe   Weren't you scheduled to continue on to China?

Jean   Yes, that's correct. Early on I had planned to do just that. But as I started to say, it wasn't that I changed my mind. It was more like I was of two minds; one was my old carefree self, and the other a new person who suddenly found purpose in life—being with General MacArthur. I was fascinated by the man and very fond of him. I've had those feelings before, many times. However, there was something different this time. Some might think I'm a frivolous person. I suppose I am a bit, but deep down I'm very serious. I take my faith very seriously; I am steeped in patriotism, and have always felt God has a plan for me to do something important.

Bobbe   I see. It appears you have now realized your purpose in life by marrying Douglas, but I must ask if you really know what you may be in for, as an Army wife?

Jean   Yes, I believe I do. My family has a very deep and abiding military service tradition. I am aware of the many difficulties and hardships a military wife must bear, and I am ready to serve my General. You know, he has discussed this very topic with me. He told me about a particular young lady he was courting many years ago. He was interested in marrying her, but he felt obliged to explain to her in detail the trials and tribulations of Army life.

He actually wrote a long poem to her, some of which he recited to me from memory. Very impressive. Like a Greek tragedy, but beautiful.

Bobbe   Did he ever tell you what happened to that young lady?

Jean   *(She laughs)* He said she ran off to Europe to get away from him!

Bobbe   But his poem of travail didn't dissuade you?

Jean   Not in the least. It made me more committed. I don't mean to get maudlin or overly sentimental, but my marriage to the General goes beyond the usual bonds of matrimony. For me our union is also a Divine vocation.

Douglas enters stage right.

Bobbe   Well, all I can say to that is, God bless you, Jean MacArthur. Oh, look! Here comes the General. *(Pause)* Douglas! It's so nice to see you. You are looking so radiant. My, my!

Douglas   And a heartfelt hello to you. *(He bends down and gives Bobbe a kiss on the cheek, then sits)* It's great to see you under these glorious circumstances.

Bobbe   *(Flustered by the kiss)* Well, I must tell you, Jean, he's never done that before. He must feel very secure being married to you. *(She gains her composure)* Please take a seat. Douglas, you <u>do</u> look like a new man since I last saw you.

Douglas	I'm like the resurrected Lazarus, thanks to this God-sent angel. *(Jean looks down demurely)*
Bobbe	Before I get totally carried away with this excitement, if you'll allow, I'd like to mention something serious that has taken place since our last meeting, the passing of your mother.
Douglas	*(He sighs and settles into his seat)* Thank you, Bobbe, for your kind remembrance. Yes, my dear mother has gone to the heavenly place. You knew how close we were. I don't know of another mother and son who had such a meaningful and loving bond for so many years. *(Near tears)* I miss her terribly, but God is so good to me. As He took away the one most dear, He sent this angel, not in her place, but like Adam's gift, to be my mate.
Bobbe	You make it sound like a fairy tale. For the two of you, it's the beginning of a new life. Isn't it?
Douglas	Yes, Bobbe. I'm quite certain it will be.
Bobbe	I don't mean to curb your enthusiasm, General, but you have completed your service with the Army. Is your appointment as Marshal of the Philippines more than an honorary position?
Douglas	Yes, it certainly is. I have a very important job to do in the Philippines, and Jean and I will be leaving soon. Furthermore, situations are developing in the world today that could very well threaten the future existence of our civilization. There are exciting and challenging chapters ahead for all of us.

Bobbe   My goodness, you are speculating far beyond my purview. May I get back to something more personal? Tell me more about your courtship and betrothal. After you met, Jean stayed on in the Philippines for about a year. Did you become engaged at that time?

Douglas No. Please understand, Mother had recently died. I was in a period of grieving. Thank God Jean was there to comfort me. At that point I had regretfully accepted the life of bachelorhood. I loved Jean from the moment we first met, but I've had so many disappointments, and under the circumstances of my mother's condition, I dared not allow my hopes to blossom.

Bobbe   How about you, Jean? How did you feel? Spending a year in, let's face it, <u>not</u> the most glamorous place in the world.?

Jean   Oh, my dear, you make it sound dreadful. It was not like that at all. Although for much of the time we contended with the sorrow of Mrs. MacArthur's decline and death, it was—I hope this doesn't sound too strange—the happiest time of my life.

Bobbe   Did you know that Douglas—as he said—did not consider himself marriageable at the time?

Jean   Yes, we discussed it, but I trusted that nature would take its course in due time. When two people love each other, even while having to deal with more consuming matters, faith sustains them and hope abounds.

Bobbe   I suppose so. What was your status when Douglas left for the States and you stayed on in the Philippines?

Jean   *(She looks at Douglas)* It was uncertain, I thought.

Douglas   I must confess I was preoccupied with military business, which was the primary purpose for this trip . . . and with my mother's burial. I was accompanying her body back to America. Once aboard and rested, however, I realized I may have made an irretrievable blunder, leaving Jean behind as I did. I missed her terribly and feared the worst. Can you imagine my delight when she greeted me at Honolulu? She had flown ahead and surprised me.

Bobbe   That was resourceful of you, Jean. Did you really know what you were doing?

Jean   No, I was scared to death he wouldn't be pleased to see me. But when he took me in his arms, I knew I had done the right thing. Then, during those days when we sailed to San Francisco, we had time to bare our hearts and souls; to really know and enjoy one another. It was marvelous!

Bobbe   Had he proposed by this time?

Jean   No, he had not. He still had unfinished business to deal with and I didn't press him. We parted company in San Francisco. He went to New York and I went home to Tennessee.

Bobbe   What happened next?

Douglas   After mother was laid to rest and my business was completed, all I could think of was Jean. I called her and asked her to come to New York as soon as possible so we could be married. That was only a week ago.

Bobbe   What was your reaction, Jean?

Jean   Oh. *(She chuckles)* I was a nervous wreck, practically sitting by the phone every day, praying he would call. Since I had no other interests at the time, I just kept packing and repacking my clothes. I tried to be ladylike and restrain myself when he called, but when he asked me to New York to marry him, I'm afraid I acted like an enthusiastic schoolgirl.

Douglas   And I loved it. You have no idea what this woman has done for me.

Bobbe   Well, dear friends, my congratulations again. I wish you *bon voyage* and a happy life in the Philippines.

End of interview

Epilogue: Douglas's Mother, Mary Pinkney MacArthur, frequently lived with, or in, close proximity to her youngest son, Douglas. Her persuasive influence strongly affected almost every aspect of his life. She was living with him in the Philippines at the time of her death in 1935.

Interview
14
Douglas & Jean

1951

Suite of Mr. & Mrs. Douglas MacArthur
Waldorf Astoria Towers, New York City

Announcer   The MacArthurs, with a small entourage—their
             long time household helper, Ah Cheu, aide
             Colonel Laurence E. Bunker, and Arthur's tutor,
             Mrs. Phyllis Gibbons—returned to America. The
             MacArthurs took up residence here at the Waldorf
             Astoria in New York City. Bobbe has come for
             an interview.

*The General's aide invites Bobbe to take a seat near the window
which looked out onto Broadway.*

Bobbe   *(To audience)* It was 1937 when I last saw the
            MacArthurs during their honeymoon; they were
            on their way to the Philippines. Tremendous
            changes have taken place these past 14 years,
            most notably WW II and now the Korean War.
            During these conflicts, General MacArthur played
            a pivotal role as one of our country's greatest
            military leaders. At the same time he nurtured a
            family; his dear wife Jean and their son Arthur IV.

Douglas enters, Bobbe stands and takes his hand.

Douglas   So many years, Bobbe. So much has happened.
            How are you?

Bobbe   I am well, General. *(She looks with concern at
            him)* And how are you? You've been through so
            much!

Douglas   I am fine, really. I'm still coming down from the
            shock of our sudden return, but it's good to be
            home at last. Please be seated, Bobbe.

Bobbe   And how about Jean, and young Arthur?

Douglas   They are wonderfully well. I believe you'll see
            Jean later.

Bobbe   I understand we cannot talk about politics and the war. You'll be testifying before Congress soon?

Douglas   Yes, and I will also have an opportunity to speak to the American people from the joint houses of Congress. It will be on television—an entirely new media since I was here last.

Bobbe   Yes, it is. How exciting! Douglas MacArthur on TV. I'll be watching intently along with millions of other Americans. Now, can I ask what your reaction is to suddenly find your career has ended and you are back in America?

Douglas   As you can imagine, I was shocked, especially to learn of my dismissal from a broadcast report. I won't go into detail, but I confess there was a measure of disappointment and despair. There was also a sense of relief. The old warrior was sad and weary when we left Tokyo. *(Pauses)* But, when we were greeted so enthusiastically by millions of Americans all across the country, my spirit soared once again. *(Now beaming)* God bless the American people for their warmth and understanding.

Bobbe   I witnessed the ticker-tape parade here in New York. It was tremendous. There has never been anything like it, not even Lindbergh's return. You must have been proud.

Douglas   And humbled, Bobbe. For as long as I live I will never forget the roar of that welcoming crowd.

Bobbe   What's next, after this government business? Maybe President?

Douglas   No, Bobbe. I have thought about it at times past; I believe I could be a fine President, but that's behind me now. I just want to spend my remaining years with Jean and Arthur.

Bobbe   I can't imagine you ever slowing down. You still look very fit for your age; in your seventies I believe. I'll be keeping my eye on you, Douglas.

Douglas   I welcome your attention, Miss Waters. Now I must excuse myself. I see Jean is here.

Douglas leaves, and Jean arrives, stage right.

Bobbe   Mrs. MacArthur. How nice to see you again.

Jean   Hello, Bobbe. You must call me Jean, or I'll fear you have forgotten me all these years.

Bobbe   I have not forgotten you at all. And I will call you Jean. You look absolutely beautiful, so radiant, so trim. You hardly look a day older than when we last met.

Jean   You are too kind. Believe me I have aged in many ways, but not a day of it would I give up, Bobbe. I must say, we are so very pleased to be back in America. We have a new life to look forward to. It's exciting.

Bobbe   I remember you saying something like that in 1937, Jean, when you and Douglas left for the Philippines. Now you are back home with the General and your son. What will young Arthur be doing? Is he looking toward West Point?

Jean   I don't think so. I'm sure his father would like to see Arthur follow the family tradition. In many ways they are cut from the same cloth, but Arthur is a sensitive lad with other interests. He has a talent for music and is quite an accomplished pianist for a 13-year-old. Even now he expresses interest in making it his career.

Bobbe   Jean, I'm certain you could write a thrilling book about your life with the General during WW II and in Japan as the Supreme Commander. But right now I'd love to hear about your personal experiences.

Jean   Oh, there is so much I could relate, but, I'll leave that for the General. He has talked about writing a book. It's his story, not mine.

Bobbe   It is certainly your story, too, and I'd love to have your personal perspective. Maybe some day in the future?

Jean   We'll see.

Bobbe   Thank you for allowing me to visit you and the General. I sincerely wish you and your family the very best, and I hope I'll be invited back into your home one day.

End of interview
(Epilogue begins on the next page)

Epilogue: In late April, 1951, General Douglas MacArthur made an address to Congress which reached millions of Americans via television. This was his famous "old soldiers never die" speech. Later he answered questions at a Congressional Committee inquiry. MacArthur was highly critical of the Truman administration's policies and was welcomed by Republicans across the country. For several months the General toured America with Jean and Arthur. People turned out by the thousands to greet him and listen to his views.

The following year, public interest shifted more to his one-time aide Dwight Eisenhower who won the Republican presidential nomination and was elected in November, 1952. Despite the change in administrations, MacArthur still did not find much support for his hard line anti-communist sentiments and geo-political views. However, he never relented in his efforts to advise the presidents, Eisenhower, Kennedy, and Johnson, of the folly and dangerous consequences of putting ground troops into battle in Asia. This advice went mostly unheeded and America gradually became involved in the infamous and most costly Vietnam War.

MacArthur finally decided to leave the running of the country to others, but he was in demand in other quarters. A number of companies felt his name, prestige, and executive talents were valuable commodities. MacArthur accepted the position of Chairman of the Board for Remington Rand and guided the merger of Sperry with the newly organized Sperry-Rand Corporation.

The Waldorf Astoria Tower became the MacArthurs' permanent home. Douglas, Jean, and Arthur were frequently seen at Broadway shows and sporting events. In 1961, the Philippine Government invited MacArthur to attend their country's 15th anniversary celebration of independence. President Kennedy, a great admirer of the General, offered a Presidential aircraft for the trip.

The MacArthurs and people of the Philippines made the most of the heralded "Sentimental Journey." The General, in an emotional discourse to the people who, for many years were the central focus of his life said he was thrilled to be back, "in the land I have loved so well, and amongst the people I have loved so well. Here I have lived my greatest moments."

A few years later, at the age of 84, MacArthur's health rapidly deteriorated. He had three operations in quick succession at Walter Reed Hospital, but he was beyond repair. General Douglas MacArthur died April 5, 1964, and was accorded the nation's highest memorial ceremonies and burial rites by President Lyndon Johnson. He was interred at the General MacArthur Memorial in Norfolk, Virginia. Louise Brooks, his first wife sent flowers. She told reporters her years with MacArthur were the happiest times of her life.

People throughout the country mourned the "old soldier," out of pure affection, or out of respect for his accomplishments. Some felt it best the General died when he did. The man was so rooted in the past, they said, he probably would not have been content to live with the changes taking place in the late 20th century.

Valley & McElhatten

Interview
15
Jean

1999

Suite of Mrs. Douglas MacArthur
Waldorf Astoria Towers, New York City

Lights are low as Jean, unseen by the audience, takes a seat next to Bobbe. As stage lights come up, we see them seated together.

Announcer   Douglas MacArthur and Jean had made their home at the Waldorf Astoria Tower from the time of their return from Japan in 1951. They did not entertain extensively, preferring periodic meeting with old friends, such as the annual get-together of Douglas's military aides and associates. For a few years, Douglas was active in business as Chairman of the Rand Corporation. After that, he contented himself primarily with his memoirs. Up until the General took sick in 1963, the MacArthurs could be seen occasionally around the city at restaurants and shows. In 1964, the General passed away. Jean moved to a smaller suite at the Waldorf-Astoria and continued her life with the support of her son Arthur, who lived elsewhere in New York City.

Bobbe   Mrs. MacArthur, it is such a delight to be with you for this very special milestone event. All best birthday wishes . . . and thank you for inviting me to your home.

Jean   Dear Bobbe, thank you for taking the time in your busy schedule to come chat with me once again. I'm not able to move about much anymore, but I did so want to see someone who has, as they say, some history with me.

Bobbe   I have such fond memories of interviewing you and General MacArthur in 1937, shortly after your wedding, and again in 1951 after you returned from Japan.

Jean   Yes. So much has happened since . . . Melancholy
            clouds form now and then when I remember my
            General has been gone for thirty-six long years.
            He, and our son, Arthur, have always been the
            balancing poles of my life.

Bobbe   Will Arthur be with you today for your Centennial
            celebration?

Jean   My son, Arthur, is a very private person and does
            not wish to have any public exposure or
            discussion of his life. I respect his request.

Bobbe   By all means. I will, as well, honor his desire for
            anonymity.

Jean   Thank you for your understanding and
            consideration.

Bobbe   I've often wondered why you didn't author a book,
            Jean? With your knowledge, love and dedication
            to the General, it would not only have been a best
            seller, but an inspiration for all military wives.

Jean   *(Shakes head)* No, dear, that's not for me. You
            know, Douglas wrote "Reminiscences," his
            memoirs, shortly before his death. I feel
            biographical material, especially that dealing with
            public figures, is difficult enough to live. The
            weight of history is truly a heavy burden—one I
            chose not to relive with the written word. It's
            better left to the professional. And the General
            was a professional in every sense. His knowledge
            of history was astounding; his mind razor sharp,
            and memory for detail always correct. He had a
            deep and abiding love of his country. He was an
            unwavering patriot.

Bobbe   That is certainly an eloquent and apt reason for leaving the writing to others. Surely though, you must often remember your life together and feel like talking about times past.

Jean   Oh, yes, but at my age I've out-lived all my contemporaries. My sentimental musings and meditations are mainly saved for confronting sleepless nights.

Bobbe   Well, we hope there are not many of those. May we ask you to share a few thoughts with us now?

Jean   I assure you it won't be very interesting—but I will say that I'm most grateful for the privileged existence I've enjoyed. Truthfully, most of my reflections are of the perilous times the General and I experienced during World War II. I recall our hasty evacuation from our home in the Manila Hotel, Christmas Eve, 1941. They were harrowing events, our lives literally in jeopardy as we moved, sometimes only hours ahead of invading forces. I do have a strong mental picture of our frightened three-year-old son, Arthur, clutching his favorite stuffed white rabbit called, "Old Friend," while being held tenderly in Douglas's arms during the bombings of Corregidor.

Bobbe   Thank you, Jean. That was certainly a poignant portrait. You've overcome so many challenges in your lifetime and your spirit seems not to have been diminished in any way.

Jean   Thank you, dear, for saying that. You know ... *(She pauses and gazes off, reflecting)* Douglas and I had a remarkably romantic partnership . . .

he gave my life meaning and encouraged me to be a realist—to accept what is, in any situation. The General often referred to me as "My Finest Soldier." With that in mind, I've always moved on with far more hope than fear to focus on the good in this world.

Bobbe   How beautifully you express your feelings. Oh, I see my time is up. I appreciate having this visit. May I leave you with these heartfelt words on your one-hundredth birthday: Jean Faircloth Mac-Arthur, you and Douglas were truly soul-mates. You complemented and completed each other— Clearly, you are the General's Woman.

End of interviews

Epilogue: Jean Marie Faircloth MacArthur's life touched three centuries, from her birth in 1899 to her death in January, 2000, at the age of 101. She was known to be gracious, warm hearted, and totally devoid of any presumptive airs. She lived alone for 36 years following Douglas's death in 1964. During that time she continued to be involved with public service work and was Honorary Chairman of the Board of Directors of the General Douglas MacArthur Foundation. In 1988, President Reagan presented the Presidential Freedom Award to Mrs. MacArthur for loyalty to her husband and her country. Mrs. MacArthur was laid to rest next to Douglas at the General Douglas MacArthur Memorial in Norfolk, Virginia, on the 120th anniversary of his birth.

Epilogue: Arthur MacArthur IV, the son and grandson of two famous generals, chooses to stay out of the public eye. It was reported, as recently as 2003, that Arthur, allegedly using another name, enjoys a relatively obscure life in New York City.

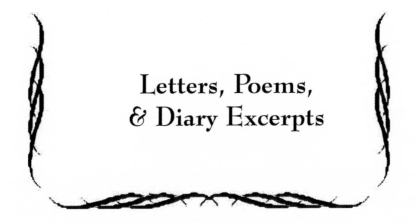

Letters, Poems,
& Diary Excerpts

Caveat

The collection of Douglas MacArthur's personal letters and poems written to the women featured in this book, along with diary entries of his written in 1904 to Florence Adams, are presented in chronological order. There is one selection not authored by Douglas: the diary entries of Florence Adams from the period of their courtship.

A review of the letters. poems, and diaries will disclose much of the source material used in the book's interviews. The authors have created dialogues based on this data. To round out the events and situations, where no details were available, the authors relied on their knowledge and understanding of the historical times and attitudes of the persons involved.

Our intent was to add only enough fiction to create a reasonable extenuation of the known facts. Others who read the detailed source material may be inclined to draw different conclusions. We sincerely feel however, that these scenarios present a valid and likely re-enactment of actual historic events.

Every precaution has been taken to correctly transcribe these documents. Please note, however, there are occasional words missing, or words may be misinterpreted from the hand written document; such words are <u>underlined</u>. The authors cannot be responsible for errors or literal misinterpretations.

Letters, Poems, and Diary Entries Regarding Miss Florence Adams

(To Florence)

Sunday Morning, October, 1904

You have been very wonderful to me in everything you have said I'm happy but how pityfully in-expressive the word becomes before the melting tenderness of the sympathy which inspired your little note.

I have been fighting it out with myself since I left you - hours and hours ago it must be but how can I fight against that?

I'm so tired that I can't even think now - but as Bill said last night, "Thank God," I have reached the stage where I can at last sleep.

No dreams will frighten me into my dark, still journey into unconsciousness, for I feel that the way will be lighted by the pale exquisite lamp of a woman's pity. If they come they will bring with them nothing but "the peace which passeth all understanding", for they will carry me far away, away from all my old Army friends, away from loving thoughts of Home, away even from my Saintly Mother - and to thy side, Sweet Florence

(Unsigned)

(To Florence)

Sunday Evening, October, 1904

There isn't the slightest excuse for this little note except to press your sweet hand and tell you how mortified - I can't say how sorry - I am at having kept you up so late last night. You have only yourself to blame though - your revenge has already been accomplished, however for all day long I have been trying to read, study, what you will, but the spell of the night still finds me. Again and again have I fallen into a midnight trance and caught myself listening with a <u>thirsty ear to the witching melody*</u> of those "wee small hours." The print on every page, in every book, every paper, I've taken up has faded away, the lines have blotted out, the pictures blurred into nothingness and left there only a sweet girl's tender eyes, until I've given it up. But strange incongruous, those very papers I lay down other's take up and even as I smile to myself at these surprise when they find what's there they read away just as if the day's news were really there. It has made me strangely afraid that they are stamped on my brain, merely mirrored and reflected on the pages through my eyes. I must be careful and let us never look into them for fear they will see there what I have been seeing.

Am I beginning to lose my head about you I wonder?

Douglas MacArthur

phrase repeated 59 years later in the General's speech at West Point.

Receipt from Douglas & Florence's last lunch

Handwritten note from Douglas on the back side of the receipt:

This certifies that being unable to meet my financial obligations I liquidate my debts—it would be true to say I increase them—by hereby certifying my soul and body to one Florence Adams—

Given under my seal
This 15th day of Oct. 1904

Signed
Douglas MacArthur
1st Corps Engr's
U.S. Army

Since Douglas was leaving the Philippines, he probably didn't have any more pesos; Florence may have paid the bill.

Diary entries of Florence Adams

The following information, primarily regarding her relationship with Lt. Douglas MacArthur, from September to October 15, 1904, details many specific activities and events. The transcription of Ms. Adams's own handwritten entries was reproduced precisely as written, with spelling errors and punctuation left uncorrected. Underlined blanks were used where hand writing was illegible and interpretation impossible.*

At Gertrude Sibling's wedding - At a Pasay hop
         on my return from Baquio - where I met him.

At the Army and Navy Club - where he recognized me when the evening was about half over   (athletic extra)

At regular Army & Navy Club where he spoke but did not ask me to dance.

At regular Army & Navy Club where I first danced with him - No. 6

At Dancing Club where I again danced with him No. 9

At seventh Inf. hop - Danced 8 & 9 with him and he brought me home.

At the Day's dance No 3 & 4

At Pasay hop next night - No 11 & 12

At 20th Inf. hop - No 3 & 4 and he asked for next Pasay hop - Thurs. He called following Sunday P.M. & found me out.

I went with him to Pasay on Thurs. I went riding with him following Tues P.M.

I went to Dancing Club with him the following Fri. night. 5 dances. On next club night I stayed at home and he came up to see me. Next day on Qugalle to lunch with him.

Next day Fri. Saw him at 7th Inf hop - one dance only   no. 2

"   "   Sat at Eda Days' for dinner & a long call with him afterward.

Not again till next Fri night - a call.

Next night (Sat) a launch party from him to Camili & a dinner.

<u>Mon</u> of the next week - a short drive in the afternoon.

<u>Tues</u> night - he called while I was away to dinner

<u>Wed</u>. afternoon - driving on the Luneta

<u>Fri</u>. <u>nig</u>ht with him to 25th dance and driving to Santa Anna - Oct 1st

Oct 2nd Sunday. A drive on the Luneta and a call in the morning.

Oct 3th Driving in the morning to the "Band concert and call afterwards.

Oct 4th Driving on Luneta.

" 5th Wed. He came down to my school and then we drove to Pasay - after dinner he called.

" 6th Driving on the Luneta.

" 7th Dancing Club and I did not see him.

" 8th He took me to the Palace to dinner.

" 9th Sunday He came to breakfast with me. We went horseback riding & he stayed all morning.

" 10th Mon. He came to my school again - & drove home with me.

Oct 11 - Tues. Driving on Luneta and a call in the evening.

" 12 - Wed - We stayed home from the Club reception together.

" 13th - Driving in the afternoon on Luneta.

" 14th, Fri Driving on Luneta & to Pandacan - and a call in the morning

" 15th - Sat. He came to lunch with me and stayed till his boat left. I went out to the boat on the launch with him.

Sunday Oct - 16th - Afternoon *(incomplete last entry)*

Diary of Douglas MacArthur
Written on board *Thomas* from Manila, P. I. to San Francisco
17 Oct - 1904 to Nov. 1904

I have always despised a diary - It is never true for one never puts into it the things to be ashamed of, and after awhile when the still small voice is silent and things are forgotten, one reads it over and says to himself, "I must have been a pretty decent chap those days," and immediately uses it for an excuse for future license.

A sort of lie to yourself it is, but I guess on the whole that kind of lie is the least dangerous of all. This diary however is going to be different, for I am not going to use it as a future salve for a troubled conscience, but am going to periodically send it away without rereading it - It should then be more or less true. I say more or less advisedly "more" meaning more true than the ordinary diary, "less," less true than the true truth.

It is but nine days since I left Manila and yet I am beginning to adjust myself to things, to fit in as it were as far as possible with the rest of the "good ships" company. But what an impossible crowd it is! I have traveled on many ships in many waters in my life but never yet have I met such a hash, such a melange, as you have to digest on the "Thomas." The most famous characteristic of Gen. Geo. H. Thomas, whose name the boat bears, was his dogged ability to hold his ground against any odds. So strickingly was this demonstrated that he was known as the "Rock of Chicamauga" after his desperate resistance on that bloody field. And yet yesterday when I was writing in the salon just under that great man's picture and that horde of petticoats, deployed and_____ loved in battle array, charged in close column on us, I distinctly saw his arm rise and point towards the door, and I could almost swear his lips whispered the warning word "run." It may have been the cocktail I had had, or it may have been my eyes going back on me, but I wasn't taking any chances of being court martialed for disobedience of orders I just "signed." But never mind, as I said before, I am beginning to fit in, and this morning after "bracing my courage with slow gin" picked out the only sweet looking girl of the bunch and sidled up to her just about the way a sick kitten sidles up to a wet brick. It is an old saying that Republics are ungrateful and unjust and now I believe it. My old Dad received the medal of honor during the Civil War for merely leading a forlorn hope against a Rebel battery, while I - I go undecorated. Ah - Justice. Rightly do they paint you blind.

I have just found out that my girl was a nursemaid who takes care of the little children on board.

I guess I'm fitting in all right. I might have guessed it though, for she was really quite clever and attractive. Tomorrow, after properly Scotching up my courage, I'm going to pick out the oldest, ugliest looking woman on board and talk my prettiest to her - There is a native tribe in the interior of Tibet whose greatest work of bravery is the wearing of a simple little piece of red cord around the right wrist. With those beggars bravery is the rule, not the exception, so brave indeed is the man who can boast that simple little "Red Badge of Courage" At the end of this voyage after I have "fitted in" for twenty more days, I'm going to buy a little piece of red cord and tie it around my wrists - not the right one only, but both. The Knocker's Club will now temporarily adjourn.

Last night was a rather gay one and as usual I broke one of my principles, namely not to play poker with women. I had been studying until midnight when I drifted into the smoking room and found this gay little party gambling their lives away, three men and two of the young grass widows on board. They insisted I join them in a little supper which became rather dizzy before the finish. One of them then proposed to reopen the game and hold an all night session. I saw I was in for it but it was too late to back out then. It is ruinous to play poker with a woman for not only does it spoil your game for playing in real earnest, but also it is difficult to lose to her without awakening her suspicions that you are deliberately doing so. Last night I held some of the most remarkable hands I have ever seen and it was one of the nastiest jobs I've tackled in a long time getting rid of my earnings. I finally did so, however, for which I'm truly thankful, for I don't think that ever I could stand taking a woman's money. By the time we stopped the game it had kicked up quite a sea and before tumbling in I went out to the bow where the wind was blowing great guns. I was drenched to the skin *muy pronto* but it did me good. With wind and wave to dissipate the hot fetid odors of smoke and champagne, and the clean sweet thought of you to purge my mind, I was able to keep to the narrow path which led to my bed and not to the orgy the crowd had started in the Doctor's stateroom. How chrystalline must be your purity when the mere thought of it can hold me straight in such a situation

The day began with a disaster. My boon companion, Leslie Holcomb, aged four years two months, dropped overboard the little gun we had gotten for him in Japan. He is a manly little fellow and has a quaint touch of saluting an officer before speaking to him. As soon as the gun went over he rushed to the Captain's cabin where a bridge game was in progress, saluted and reported the loss.

Such a ludicrously pathetic little boy it was but the Captain rose to the situation like a great man. Not a sign of a smile was on his lips as he rose, gravely returned the salute and asked me to present his compliments to the Officer of the Deck with instructions to take every possible means to rescue the lost gun. We played it through as far as lowering one of the boats half way, but the sea being rough, the Captain, Leslie and myself after a deep consultation on the bridge decided that the attempt would be hopeless. Poor little chap - His lip quivered so when he saluted and said good bye to the Captain. I'm going to get him the best gun in Honolulu if I have to become bankrupt.

I'm lonesome, horribly lonesome for you these long days and of all sensations I have experienced it is the worst. I can't fight it off for it presents nothing tangible to fight, I can't get away from it because it is internal, and I can't deceive it by trying to make others fill in the gap, for although you can "deceive some of the people all of the time, and all of the people some of the time" there are two beings you can never deceive any of the time your God and, as in this case, yourself. I'm not exactly following Leslie's example, I know, to go mooing around like a love sick calf - but I guess I'm the calf all right. If I had only stayed over until November - and do you know I came within an ace of not being allowed to sail even after I was on board. It seems they crossed my name off the passenger list at two o'clock and the quarantine people having cleared her at that time refused to "rectify the _____ without some good excuse. I hauled out my letter from the Q.M. on them but this did not satisfy their mighty lordships and they enquired as to the reason for the letter, and when I told them in a very solemn way that I had been subpoened as an interested party in the court of love, they had the nerve to say I had been drinking. Pretty rough that, wasn't it? Made me mad clean through. Before, I had been perfectly willing to get off and had even asked my _____ to get my trunks together for that purpose but after that remark I "made up my mind to sail away." It was a game of bluff nothing more, nothing less, so I gave them all the fireworks they could digest. The Q.M. finally weakened when I told him I intended to prefer charges and I was allowed to _____ Now, after the storm of battle has rolled by I realize "how dumb slow" I was not to eat a little humble pie and stay with you another month. Who was it that said the saddest thing on Earth next to a great defeat is a great victory.

Good night, Sweet Child. May I take you in my arms just once and tell you very softly I love you - love you - love you?

Just a year ago today I landed in Manila. I didn't think at that time I would celebrate the anniversary homeward bound. But Uncle Sam is an uncertain master. Isn't the charm of Army life, however, in this very uncertainity.

Life on board goes on in the same old rut. I have ceased trying to fill in and pass my time as the humor seizes me. A little reading, a little studying, a little snooze, and a call on the General fills in the day, a poker game keeps me going till the wee small hours. I don't say you will hold up your hands in horror at this last but do not judge me too harshly. In one sense the game is truly a root of evil, but in another, it becomes, to my mind, entirely legitimate. When the gamester plays not for the pleasure of sensations involved, but for the capital he hopes to win, he ceases to be a mere recreation seeker, and becomes an out and out gambler, which is merely a referred name for robber. A person that tries to get something for nothing. But, on the other hand, when a person with just so much money in his pocket which he is willing to lose and beyond which he will not go, that is, one who will play until he loses just so much, then stop, - enters the game he merely purchases the amusement of the sport for the money involved. A business transaction, pure and simple, which parallels the purchasing of a ticket to the opera, the ball game or anything of that sort. If instead of losing he wins, it is merely incidental. It is his friend across the table who purchases the tickets for that evening. Instead of being host, he is guest.

Bad dreams again last night. I am beginning to dread sleep. This time it was those rascally Apaches who came so near getting me some fifteen years ago. We were hiding, you and I, and they had passed us by. When strange, horrible to me, you called to them where I was. And they came and got me, those red devils, and tied me hand and foot, and then strange trick of an unconscious mind, it seemed to me you sailed away with them in a little launch with the red castle up on the bow, and a smile on your lips. I must have shouted your name for when I woke up with my bunker's hand on my shoulder, there was that in his eyes which told me he knew. And his touch and his voice were tender as a womans as he said "time to tumble out, old man" - Ah - the infinite tact of friendship! It was just after four in the morning and ordinarily he gets up about nine.

The last four days have slipped by without any record herein. It has been the same old tale for me, poker all night, sleep all morning, bridge all afternoon. An itinerary I'm not proud of in the least, but one that keeps me busy and from thinking about you. I'd do things much worse than that to get away from those horrible dreams of mine.

We had our first death on Monday. It was a stowaway from Manila. I was present at the operation due to the courtesy of the surgeon. He went down after an abscess. but didn't get it. Just before he died the man sent for me. Said he didn't have a friend in the world but if I didn't mind he'd like to think I was one. Said it would help him to die decently and like he had been born but not lived, a gentleman. He went off in his head just before the end, and babbled of strange men and women whom he had loved in his stormy life, before he reached the bottom of the ladder. At the last he thought I was his mother and died in my arms peaceably like a little child, with such a smile on his face and her name on his lips. Poor devil - I hope his path is easier in the next world than in this.

We get in tomorrow - I have made no entrys in this record for the past ten days, partly because there has been little out of the ordinary, partly through fear that this whole thing will be but dry reading for you. I am going to send these pages on, however, for each line, each word is full of my love for you.

We have cast anchor in the harbor but too late to be cleared. I can see the lights twinkling in the windows of our house, but, pity me, Child, for even with those beacons lighting me home I could curse the fate that has brought me back and from you.

End of MacArthur's journal entries

November, 1904

My Sweet Child:

I wish I had the power to adequately express my thoughts of and to you. They would be so exquisitly tender, so reverentially loving, that all other lovers reading would feel a pang that their love was such a starveling thing compared to mine. Do I hear you laugh, Sweetheart, that rippling infectious laugh, which always had its birth in your eyes but whose echo still rings in my heart? As always the mere thought of it makes me smile in sympathy, a smile which will end in a sob of lonliness and longing for you. It has been a thousand times worse for me than I thought it would be. I feel like a man who has been under the knife, but instead of losing a leg or an arm, my very soul seems to have been taken out. Unconsciously, I hear my lips forming the words wrung from Jesus Christ in his hours of agony "How long, O God, how long." Do I sound wild, incoherent, extravagant? Perhaps, but bear with me.

We have been cleared and I see the tug which brings the family just off the port bow. It is goodbye, little girl, for a few days   But remember that I am thinking of you always. I understand I am to stay at Frisco so address me   Ft. Mason - San Francisco - <u>Cal</u>

January, 1905

Tonight, sweetheart, the sun unrolled
Across the bay a path of gold.
And in the glory of that track
I sent a lonesome wanderer back,
A burning thought to thee.
Sweet Child, be on the watch tonight
Between the sunset and moonlight
Perhaps my thoughts will come to rest
And seek repose upon thy breast,
When the long, dreary day is done

Dear Lady of Dreams, the days seem long
And sweet sad memories round her throng.
Those happy summer hours are past
And darkness shrouds my life at last.
Illumined once by thee.

Will you take this New Year's greeting from me with all my love? No
word from you since I left the Islands, but last night at the Club I joined
heartily in a New Year's toast - "Here's hopeing."

Douglas

Letters to Lucretia LeBourgeois

April 30, 1907

Lucretia Dear Child

This is just a line to pass onto your sweet hand. It has been a ghastly long evening for me... my only consolation the knowledge that from the instant I left you, every minute that drops by brings me so much nearer.

The wild spell has been with me again and all night long. I have been fighting it out with myself to keep from going to you like a thief in the night. Too late now, you must have been asleep there many hours—but I can bespeak you at least sweet dreams. Mine will be so, for I know they will carry me across the broad stretch of Washington town—and to thy side—sweet lady."

Douglas

May 8, 1907

My Sweet Child

 There is little to write of from these gloomy barracks, save to tell you the old, old story—I love you. I love you—love you. How many countless millions in every land, in every age have used the same phrase. And yet, as I whisper it to you now, how poignant with meaning, how heavy with memories the words seem to be.

I am desperately tired and sick of everything about me tonight. Even my ride today has failed to drive away the 'little blue devils'—on my way back I lingered by the river until sunset. There were just enough clouds to make it beautiful and I sat on the bluff above and watched for it. Purple and gold and azure and crimson change to opal and gray—and at last in a wondrous glow to blind the eyes, the sun went down in a flood of molten gray—the river trembled into shadow, then into twilight and finally dark. And thus it has been with me. My sun is down. Shadows are all about, and dark star night is reaching out for me. But through my window Avon ways to the north. I can see upraised on a slender pillar of white cloud, the fain exquisite lamp of a star.

Douglas

May 31, 1907

Lucretia Sweetheart

The mailman visited me a few moments ago and in consequence I have learned of your safe arrival and disagreeable passage. Beastly trip it must have been and I sympathize greatly with My Sweet "little friend."

You are haunting me. Not a bird sings under my window but carols your name—not a breeze stirs the leaves but whispers of you—Not a wind in the storm last night but moaned out "Lucretia, Lucretia." You make work impossible. I see you everywhere.

My books blur—the lines fade into nothingness, the words blot out—and your lips smile at me. Not a light in the house but reflects the sparkle of your dark eyes. I even fear to let people look into mine, lest they see you there. I feel tonight I could curse God, I miss you so much, you could not be quite happy did I tell you how much.—

Douglas

June 14, 1907

The mailman came to camp today and brought me your violets. This faint delicate fragrance reminds me of you, as what beautiful thing does not. I close my eyes and put my face down to them and—Lo—your sweet lips are smiling back at me, your soft hand groping for mine. It is a greater gift than the giver gave in the older times, for the talisman brought nothing but gold and precious stones. Unfailing tenderness brings in the vision of you.

I was out here in camp these days in charge of a big survey party. Twenty one they number and a nice lot of boys they are. Most of them just out of some university and getting their first practical experience. Enthusiastic and loyal, my task of directing their work is merely pleasant recreation. And at night they come to my tent, and build their little camp fire and they gather around me and I tell them of the old days on the plains, when I was a little boy, of life as a vaquero, of cadet days, of the Philippines, of China, India, Siam, of battles and camps and fights—but never do I tell them what is at war in my mind—the memory of your sweet, serious eyes. And they drop off one by one to tumble into bed, dear children, and at last I am left alone by the dead embers of the fire with only my thoughts of you. And I drop off into a midnight trance in which I listen again with a thirsty ear to the witching melody of the days that are gone.

Douglas

June 24, 1907

Home again—if you can call four walls and a club a home. And that—now that you are gone— is all that Washington means to me. It is beautiful, though, in all the greenness of new spring and a relief to one's eyes from dirty Pittsburgh town. A desolate place is the latter with little to attract one. Not even in its brightest moments could it be accused of giddiness. It is a study in half-tones— nothing to relieve the dreary monotony of the daily routine, absolutely no form of amusement. Night brings to the youth of the place only bed and boredom. There is no pleasurable place between deviltry and stolen conversationability.

I leave it after a week's stay with little more than a memory of blackbread, locusts, a sooty sky—and the mailman. The Hee-Haw Pittsburger, however drinks his 'strength' at his club, rolls up his trousers when it rains, and he is a 'devil of a fellah." I have built me a fire tonight in my old open grate—not that it is cold, but it reminds me so of you. How like, too, it is for you—a fire. The sparkle of it, your nimble wit, the warmth, your sweet tenderness enveloping softly everything within its radius—the glow, the light that lies in the bottom of your eyes. And the gold of it, which is like nothing in this wide, wide world but you loyal true heart.

Douglas

Valley & McElhatten

Poems to Fannibelle Stuart

January 29, 1908

Why Not?

Fair Gotham girl

With life a whirl

Of dance and fancy free,

'Tis thee I love—All things above

Why cans't thou not love me?

Valley & McElhatten

February 24, 1908

The House of Dreams

I live in a little house of dreams
In a land that cannot be—
The country of the fain desire,
That I shall never see—
Save with the waking eyes of dreams,
The land that cannot be.

Why should I tell of my house of dreams?
You have been with me there
You know the walls of joy and pain
And you did not find them fair.
My little dusky house of dreams,
Dark with your hanging hair—

You have kissed our little children's lips
And held them on your knee,
My little dream boy has your smile,
He is so dear to me—
His eyes are lit by the strange light
Not seen on land or sea—

I close the door to my house of dreams
Lest the eyes of the world might see
What is far too pure for an earthly eye,
A dream love's ecstasy—
So I close the door to my house of dreams
In the land that cannot be.

The unsigned, untitled document presented in the following pages is in the handwriting of Douglas MacArthur. It was addressed to Miss Fannibelle Stuart, 71 Central Park West, New York City, NY. She apparently was no longer at that address and the letter was forwarded to the Regina Hotel, Paris, France. The return address was: War Department, United States Engineer Office, P.O. Drawer 7, Milwaukee, Wisconsin. The prose is proceeded by the introduction that follows. The authors of this book have given this epic poem the title: Wife of an Army Man. Special thanks to Mary Lenore Quigley who transcribed the second half of this poem. (Note that underlined words were difficult to decipher and represent the best guess of the transcriber.)

April 17, 1908

Fannie

Read this jingle and you will know why my heart sinks at the thoughts of ever bringing into realty the heartbreak of the dreams I have woven.

I have tried to picture a little of the life and of the fate of Army women— Of what might be your lot if you should ever decide to don the Army Blue.

It is only after much hesitation that I have forced myself to do this, for I feel that it probably takes away even my fighting chance. Too many women, though, join us without a realization of what it all may mean. So, in the spirit of fair play, I give you this peek at my probable destiny.

Wife of an Army Man

(Written to Fannibelle Stuart)

There is sorrow at home;—brightly the day
Has beamed with the earliest glory of May;
The blue of the sky is as tender a blue
As ever the sunshine came shimmering through.
The songs of the birds and the hum of the bees,
As they merrily dart in and out of trees,
The blooms of the orchard, as sifting its snows
It mingles its odors with hawthorn and rose—
The voice of the brook, as it lapses unseen—
The laughter of children at play on the green—
Insist on a picture so cheerful, so fair,
Whoever would dream that a grief could be there.

The last yellow sunbeam slides down from the wall,
The purple of evening is ready to fall;
The gladness of daylight is gone, and the gloom,
Of something like sadness is over the room.
Right bravely all day, with a smile on her brow
Miss Fan ever true to her duty—but now
Her tasks are all ended—naught inside or out
For the thought fullest love to be busy about;
The knapsack well furnished, the canteen all bright
The soldier's blue dress and his <u>guantlets</u> in sight
The blanket tight strapped, and the haversack store,
And lying beside them, the cap and the sword;
No last, little office—no further command
No service to steady the tremulous hands;
All wife work—the sweet work that busied her so
Is finished:—the dear one is ready to go.

The General's Women

Not a sob has escaped her all day —not a moan;
But now the tide rushes, for she is alone.
On the fresh shining knapsack she pillows her head,
And weeps as a mourner might weep for the dead.
Around the young body there suddenly press
The arms of her husband with loving caress,
And fast to his heart—love and duty at strife—
He snatches, with fondest emotion, his wife.

"My own love! My precious!—I feel I am strong;
I exult in the thought of opposing the wrong.
I could stand where the battle was fiercest, not feel
One quiver of nerve at the flash of the steel;
I could smile while you wrought for me—mock
At your fears, but I quail at the sight of these passionate tears.
My cleverness forsakes me—my thoughts are a-whirl,
And my usual stout heart is as weak as a girl's.
I've been proud of your fortitude; never a trace
Of yielding all day, could I read in your face;
But a look that was resolute, dauntless and high,
As ever flashed forth from a Patriot's eye.
I know how it hurts you—know that to part
Is tearing the tenderest chords of your heart:
Through the length and the breath of our Land today,
No hand with a costlier sacrifice lay
On the Alter of Country; and Fan—sweet wife
I never have worshipped you so in my life.
Poor heart that has held up so brave in the past—
Poor heart! Must it break with its burden at last.

Valley & McElhatten

The arms thrown about him tightened their hold,
The cheek that he kisses is ashy and cold,
And bowed with the grief she so long has suppressed,
She weeps herself quiet and calm on his breast.
At length, in a voice just as steady and clear,
As if it had never been choked by a tear,
She raises her eyes with a softened control,
And through them her husband looks into her soul.

"I feel that we each for the other could die,
Your heart to my own makes the instant reply,
But dear as you are, Love, - my life and my light,
I would not consent to your stay if I might;
No! – arm for the conflict, and on, with the rest,
Wisconsin has need for her bravest and best!
My heart—it must bleed, and my chest will be wet,
Yet never believe me with selfish regret:
My ardor abates not one jot of its glow,
Though the tears of the wife and the woman must flow."

She pauses a moment; the white rose on her breast
Is heaved by the sob which the heart has repressed;
Love pleads, as a swimmer that's drowning, for life,
Yet vanity—the <u>heroics</u> conquers the wife.

"Our cause is so holy, so just, and so true—
Thank God! I can give—for freedom—for bread—
For the house of our God—for the graves of our dead—
For leave to exist on the soil of our birth—
For everything manhood holds dearest on earth:
When these are the things we fight for—dare I
Hold back my dear treasure, with plaint or with sigh?

The General's Women

My cheek would blush crimson—my spirit be galled
If you were not there when the muster was called!
I grudge you not, Douglas—die, rather than yield,
And like the old heroes, come home on your shield!

The morning is breaking:—the flush of the dawn
Is waking the soldier, 'tis time to be gone;
The children around him expectantly wait;
His horse, all comparisoned, paws at the gate:
With face strangely pallid—no sobbing, no sighs—
But only a luminous mist in her eyes,
His wife is subduing the heart throbs that swell,
And calming herself for a quiet farewell.
The little ones each he has caught to his breast,
And clasped them and kissed them with fervent caress:
Then wordless and tearless, with hearts running o'er
They part who have never been parted before;
He springs to his saddle—the rein is drawn tight,
And Home is quickly lost to his sight.

II

There is quiet at home; sweet Fan's brow
Is wearing a Sabbath tranquility now,
As softly she reads from the page on her knee,
"Thou wilt keep him in peace who is stayed upon Thee!"

When Belle burst breathlessly into the room,
"Oh Mother! We hear it! We hear it!"—The boom
Of the fast and the fierce cannonading!—it shook
The ground 'til it trembled, along by the brook.

149

Valley & McElhatten

One instant the listener sways in her seat—
The paralyzed heart has forgotten to beat;
The next, with the spud and the frenzy of fear,
She gains the green hillock, and pauses to hear.

Again and again the reverberant sound
Is fearfully felt in the tremulous ground;
Again and again on their senses it thrills,
Like thunderous echoes astray in the hills.

For her, all silent and motionless stands,
And over her heart locks her quivering hands,
With blanched lips apart, and with eyes that dilate
As if the low thunder were sounding her fate—
What racking suspenses, what agonies stir,
What specters these echoes are rousing for her!
Brave-natured, yet quaking—high-souled, yet so pale,
Is it thus that the wife of a soldier should quail,
And shutter and shrink at the boom of a gun,
As only a faint-hearted girl should have done?
Ah! Wait until custom has blunted the pun
Cutting edge of that sound, and no woman I swear
Will hear it with pulse more equal, more free
From feminine terrors and weakness than she.

The sun sinks serenely; a lingering look
He flings at the mists that steal over the brook,
Like news that comes forth in the twilight to pray,
Till their blushes are seen through their mantels of gray.
The gay-hearted children, but lightly opprest,
Find perfect relief on their pillow of rest:

The General's Women

For Fan, no kindly forgetfulness comes;—
The wail of the bugles—the roll of the drums—
The musket's sharp crack—the artillery's roar—
The flashing of bayonets dripping with gore—
The moans of the dying—the horror, the dread,
The ghastliness gathering over the dead—
Oh! These are the visions of anguish and pain—
The phantoms of terror that troop through her brain.

She pauses again and again on the floor
Which the moonlight has brightened so mockingly o'er
She wrings her cold hands with a groan of despair,
"Oh God! Have compassion—my loved one is there.

All placidly, devily, freshly, the dawn
Comes stealing on pulse less tranquility on:
More freely she breathes, in its balmyness, though
The forehead it kisses is pallid with woe.

Through the long summer sunshine the cottage is <u>eternal</u>
<u>By passers</u> who brokenly fling them a word;
"Such tiding of slaughter! The evening cowers;"—
"He breaks!—He is flying!" "The victory is ours."
'Tis evening: and Arthur, alone on the grass,
Sits watching the fireflies gleam as they pass,
When sudden he rushes, too eager to wait—
"Momma! there's an ambulance stops at the gate;
Suspense then is passed: he is borne from the field—
"God help me!—God grant it be not on his shield.
And Fan, her passionate soul in her eyes,
And hope and fear winging each quicken'd step, flies
Embraces with frantic wildness the form
Of her husband, and finds—it is living and warm.

Valley & McElhatten

III

Ye, who by the couches of languishing ones,
Have watched through the rising and setting of suns,
We, silent, behind the close curtain, withdrawn,
<u>Seare</u> know that the current of being <u>swepson</u>—
To whom outer life is unreal, untrue,
A world with whose toils you have nothing to do,
Who feel that the day, with its multiforum trends,
Is full of discordant, impertinent sounds—
Who speak in low whispers, and stealthily tread,
As if a faint footfall is something to dread—
Who find all existence—its gladness, its gloom—
Enclosed by the walls of that limited room—
Ye only can measure the sleepless unrest,
That lies like a nightmare on Fan's sweet breast.
Days come and days goes, and she watches the strife
So evenly balanced, 'twixt death and 'twixt life;
Thanks God he still breathes, as each evening takes wing,
And dares not to think what tomorrow may bring.

In the lone, ghostly midnight, he raves as he lies,
With death's ashen pallidness dimming his eyes:
He shouts the sharp warcry—he rallies his men—
He is on the red field of battle again.
"Now courage, my lads! Keep steady! lie low!
Wait, you young devils, to spring for your foe.
Come on, when I call, to the cannons grim mouth,
And my brave Yankee ladies, we'll put 'em to route.
Follow me close—with a cheer and a yell,
And we'll drive those brown beggars clear into hell!

The General's Women

Be ready my bullies—We'll turn 'em—and then
We'll ride 'em down madly" Oh! Onward my men!"
The feverish frenzy o'er wearies him soon,
And back on his pillows he sinks in a swoon,
But Nature, kind healer! Brings sou'reingnest balm,
And strokes the wild pulses with coolness and calm;
The conflict so equal, so stubborn is past,
And life gains the hardly won battle at last.

How sweet through the long convalescence to be,
And from the low window, gaze out at the sea,
While thought, floating aimless as summer winds down
Is lost in the depths of ineffable blue:—
In painless half-consciousness brood
No duties to cumber, no claims to intrude—
Receptive as childhood, from trouble as free,
And feel it is bliss enough, simply to be!

For Fan, - what pencil can picture her joy—
So perfect, so thoughtful, so free from annoy,
As her lips press the lotus—bound chalice and drain
That exquisite blessedness born out of pain!
Not in her maidenhood, blushing and sweet,
When Douglas first poured out his love at her feet;
And not when a striking and beautiful bride,
With tenderest fondness she clung to his side;
And not in those holiest moments of life,
When first she was held to his heart, as his wife,
And never in motherhood's earliest bliss,
Had she tasted a happiness rounded like this!

Valley & McElhatten

And Douglas, safe sheltered from war's rude alarms,
Finds Eden's lost precincts again in her arms:
He hears afar off, in the distance, the roar
And the lash of the billows that break on the shore
Of his isle of enchantment,—his haven of rest,—
And rapturous languor steels over his breast,
He baths in the sunlight of Fanniebelle's smiles;
He wraps himself round with love's magical smiles.
His sweet iterations pall not on her ear,—
"I love you – I love you!"— she never can hear
That cadence too often; it's musical roll
Wakes ever an echoed reply in her soul.

Do visions of trial, of warring, of woe
From dark in the future of doubt? Do they know?
They are living, of honeyed remberances, a <u>store</u>
To live on, when summer ends and sunshine is o'er?
Do they feel that their island of beauty at last
Must be rent by the tempest, - be swept by the blast
Do they dream that afar, on the wild, wintry main,
Their love-freighted bark must be driven again?
Bless God for the wisdom that curtains so tight,
Tomorrow's enjoyments or grief from our sight.
Thank God for the ignorance, darkness and doubt,
That girdle so kindly our future about!

The crutches are brought, and the invalid's strength
Is able to measure the town's gravel'd length
And under the birches once more he reclines
And hears the wind plaintively moan through the pines;
His children around him with frolic and play
Cheat Autumn's mild listlessness out of the day.
An Fan, the sunshine all flecking her book,
Reads low to the chime of the measuring brook.

154

The General's Women

An Fan, the sunshine all flecking her book,
Reads low to the chime of the measuring brook.

But the world's rushing tide washes up to his feet,
And leaps the soft barrier that bounds his retreat.
The tumult of camps surges out of the breeze,
And ever seems mocking his Captain's ease.
He dare not be happy, or tranquill, or blest,
While his soil by the feet of invaders is pressed,
What brooks it though still he be pale as a ghost
  -   If he languish or fail, let him fail at his post.

The <u>grains</u> by the brookside are crimson and brown;
The leaves of the ash flicker goldenly down;
The roses that trellis the porches, have lost
Their brightness and bloom at the touch of the frost;
The ozier-twined seats by the beeches, no more
Looks tempting, and cheerful, and sweet, as of yore
The water glides darkly and mournfully on,
As Fan sits watching it:- Douglas has gone!

IV

"I am weary and worn—I am hungry and chill,
And cuttingly strikes the keen blast o'er the hill;
All day have I ridden through snow and through sleet,
With nothing—not even a cracker to eat,
But now, as I rest by the bivouac fire,
Whose blaze leaps up merrily, higher and higher,
Impatient as Roland, who neighs to be fed,
For Caleb to bring me my bacon and bread;
I'll warm my cold heart, that is ailing and lone,
By thinking of you, love— my Fan— my own.

155

Valley & McElhatten

"I turn a deaf ear to the scream—of the <u>cried</u>
I leave the rude camp and the forest behind
And Home, wrapped in its raincoat of white,
Is tauntingly filling my vision tonight.
I catch my sweet little ones innocent mirth
I watch your dear face, as you sit at the hearth,
And I know, by the tender expression I see,
I know that my darling is musing of me.

"What brave, buoyant letter you write, sweet!— they ring
Tho' my soul like the blast of a trumpet, and bring
Such a flame to my eye, such a flush to my cheek—
That often my hand will unconsciously seek
The hilt of my sword as I read—and I feel
As the warrior does, when he flashes the steel
In fiery circles, and shouts in his might,
For the heroes behind him, to follow its light!
True wife of a soldier!—if doubt or dismay
Had ever, within me, one instant held sway,
Your words wield a spell that would bid them be gone,
Like bodiless ghosts at the touch of the dawn.

"Could the vilest craven that cowers and quails
Before the vast horde that insults and assails
Our land and our liberties—could be tonight
Sit here on the ice girdled log where I write,
And look on the hopeful, bright brows of the men,
Who have toiled all the day over mountain, through glen—
Half clothed and unfed—would he doubt?—would he dare
In the face of such proof, yield again to despair?

156

The General's Women

"The fire burned dimly, and scattered around
The men lie asleep on the snow covered ground
But ere in my blanket I wrap me to rest,
I hold you, my darling, close—close to my breast.
God love you! God grant you his comforting light
I kiss you a thousand times over—Good night!

V

The lull of the Winter is over; and Spring
Comes back, as delicious and buoyant a thing
As airy, and fairy, and lightsome, and bland
As if not a sorrow was dark'ning the land,
So little has Nature of passion or part
In the woes and the throes of humanity's heart.

The wild tide of battle runs red—dashes by
And blocks out the splendor of earth and of sky,
The blue air is heavy, and sulph'rous, and dull?
And the breeze on its wings bears the boom of the yawl?
In faster and fiercer and deadlier shocks,
The thunderous billows are hurled on the rocks,
And our valley becomes, amid Spring's softest breath,
The valley, alas! of the shadow of death.

The spirit of Fan no longer is bowed
By the troubles, and tumults, and terrors, that crowd
So closely around her, the willows lithe form
Bends meekly to meet the wild rush of the storm.

Valley & McElhatten

Yet, pale as Cassandra, unconscious of joy,
With visions of Greeks at the gates of her Troy,
All day she has waited and watched on the lawn,
Till the purple and gold of the sunset are gone.
For the battle draws near her;—few leagues intervene
Her home and that valley of slaughter, between.

The tidings and rumours come thick and come fast,
As riders fly hotly and breathlessly past;
They tell of the onslaught—the <u>headbog</u> attack
Of the foe with a quadruple force at his back.

At length, with the gradual fading of day—
The tokens of battle are floated away:
The booming no longer makes sullen the air,
And the silence of night seems as holy as prayer.
Gray shadows still linger the beeches among,
And scarce has the <u>earliest</u> nation been sung.

Ere Fan, with Arthur, pale at her side,
Yet <u>firm</u> as his Mother, is ready to ride.
With sympathy, womanly, tender, divine—
With <u>lin</u> and with bandage, with bread and with wine—
She hastens to the battlefield, eager to bear
Relief to the wounded and perishing there
To breath, like an angel of mercy, the breath
Of peace over brows that are fainting in death

The General's Women

She dares not to stir with a question, her woe;
One word - and the bitter-bruises of heart would o'erflow:
But speechless, and moveless, and story of guy
Scare conscious of aught in the earth or the sky
In a swoon of the heart, all her senses have reared
But she prays for endurance—for here is the fear

The flight and pursuit, so harassing, so hot,
Have drifted all combatants far from the spot,
And though the sparse woodlands, and over the plains,
Lie gorily scattered, the wounded and slain.
Oh! the sickness— the shudder— the quailing of fear,
As it leaps to her lips—"What if Douglas be here!"

Yet she frames not a question; her spirit can bear
Oh! anything—all things, but hopeless despair—
Does her laddie lie stretched on the slope of yon hill?
Let her doubt— let her buy. The suspense if she will.

She watches each ambulance burden with dread;
She looks in the faces of dying and dead:
And hour after hour, with steady control,
She bends to her task all the strength of her soul;
She comforts the wounded with pity's sweet care,
And the spirits that passing, she speeds with her prayer.

She starts as she hears, from her stout-hearted boy,
A wild exclamation, half doubt and half joy;
"Oh! Surgeon!—Some brandy! he's fainting!—Ah! Now

Valley & McElhatten

The color comes back to his cheek—and his brow:—
He breathes again—speaks again—listen! You are
'An orderly—is it? 'Of Colonel Macar?
"His men fought like demons! The Colonel passed
Untouched through the battle, unhurt to the last."
"My Father is safe—Mother!—safe! What joy!
This is his orderly—this poor wounded boy.

VI

"My Douglas! My darling—there once was a time
When we to each other confessed the sublime
And perfect sufficiency love could bestow
On the hearts that have learned its completeness to know;
We felt that we two had a well-spring of joy,
That earthly convulsions could never destroy—
A mossy, sealed fountain, so cool and so bright
It could solace the soul, let it thirst as it might.

"'Tis easy, while happiness strews in our path
The richest and costliest blessings it hath;
'Tis easy to say that no sorrow, no pain,
Could utterly beggar our spirits again;
'Tis easy to sit in the sunshine, and speak
Of the darkness and storm, with a smile on the cheek.

"As hungry and cold, and with weariness spent,
You droop in your saddle, or crouch in your tent,
Can you feel that the love so entire, so true,

The General's Women

The love that we dreamed of—is all things to you;
That come what there may—desolation or loss,
The prick of the thorn, or the weight of the cross—

"You can bear it—nor feel you are wholly bereft,
While the bosom that beats for you only, is left?
While the birdlings are spared that have made it so blest,
Can you look, undismayed, on the wreck of the nest?

"You guess what I Fan? Would keep hidden—you know
Ere now, that the trail of the insolent foe
Leaves ruins behind it, disastrous and dire,
And burns through our valley, a pathway of fire.
Our beautiful house—as I write it, I weep—
Our beautiful house is a smouldering heap!
And blackened, and blasted, and grim, and forlorn,
Its chimneys stand stark in the mists of the morn!

"I stood in my womanly helplessness, weak—
Though I felt a brave color was kindling my cheek—
And I plead by the sacredest things of their live—
By the love that they bore to their children—their wives,
By the houses left behind them, whose joys they had shared,
By the God that should judge them—that mine should be
spared.

"As well might I plead, with the whirlwind to stay,
As it crushingly cuts through the forest its way!
I know that my eye flashed a passionate ire,
As they scornfully flung me their answer of—fire!

Valley & McElhatten

"Why barrow your heart with the grief and the pain?
Why paint you the picture that's scorching my brain?
Why speak of the night when I stood on the lawn,
And watched the last flame die away in the dawn.
'Tis over—that vision of terror—of woe!
Its horrors I would not recall;— let them go!
I am calm when I think what I suffered them for
I grudge not the quota I pay to the war!

"But, Douglas!—deep down in the core of my heart,
There's a throbbing, an aching, that will not depart;
For memory mocks us with a wail of despair,
The loss of her treasures—the subtle, the rare,
Precious things over which she delighted to pore,
Which nothing—ah! nothing, can ever restore!

"The rose covered porch, where I sat as your bride
The hearth, where at twilight I leaned at your side
The low-cushioned window-seat, where I would like,
With my head on your knee, and look out on the sky.
The chamber all holy with love and with prayer;
The motherhood memories clustering there;
The vines that your hand has delighted to train,
The trees that you planted;—Oh! never again
Can love build us up such a tower of bliss;
Oh! Never can home be as hallowed as this!

"The children—dear hearts!—it is touching to see
My Arthur's beautiful kindness to me;

The General's Women

Not a childish complaint or regret have I heard,
Not even from Malcolm a petulant word.
A stranger I wander 'midst strangers; and yet
I never—no not for a moment, forget
That my heart has a home—just as real, as true,
And as warm as if Home sheltered me too.
God grant that this refuge from sorrow and pain
This blessed haven of peace, may remain!
And then, though disaster, still sharper, befall,
I think I can patiently bear with it all:
For the rarest, most exquisite bliss of my life
Is wrapped in a word, Douglas—I am your wife."

VII

'Tis morn—but the night has brought Fan no rest:
The roof seems to press like a weight on her breast;
And she wanders forth, wearily lifting her eye,
To seek for relief 'neath the calm of the sky.

The air of the forest is spicy and sweet,
And dreamily babbles a brook at her feet;
Her children are 'round her, and sunshine and flowers
They vainly to banish the gloom of the hours.
With a volume she fain her wild thoughts would assuage
But her vision can trace not a line on the page,
And the poet's dear strains, once so soft to her ear
Have lost all their mystical power to cheer.

Valley & McElhatten

The evening approaches; the pressure—the woe
Grows drearier—weighs heavier—yet she must go
And stifle between the dead walls, as she may,
The heart that scarce breathed in the free open <u>day.</u>

She reaches the dwelling that serves as her home
A horseman awaits at the entrance;—the foam
Is flecking the sides of his fast-ridden steed,
Who pants, over-worn with exhaustion and speed
And Fan for support to Arthur clings,
As the soldier delivers the letter he brings.

Her ashy lips move, but the words do not come,
And she stands in her whiteness, bewildered and dumb.
She turns to the letter with hopeless appeal,
But her fingers are helpless to loosen the seal:
She lifts her dim eyes with a look of despair,
Her hands for a moment are folded in prayer;
The strength she has sought is vouchsafed in her need—
"I think I can bear it now, Arthur - - - - read."

The boy with the resolute nerve of a man,
And a voice which he holds as serene as he can
Takes quietly from her the letter, and reads:—

"Dear Madam—my heart in its sympathy bleeds
For the pain that my tidings must bring you; may God
Most tenderly comfort you, under His rod!

The General's Women

"This morning, at daybreak, a terrible charge
Was made on the evening's centre: such large
and fresh reinforcements were held at his back,
He stoutly and stubbornly met the attack.

"Our cavalry bore themselves splendidly—far
In front of his line galloped Colonel MacAr;
Erect in his stirrups—his sword flashing high,
And the look of a patriot kindling his eye,
His hoarse voice rang aloft through the roar
Of the musketry poured from the opposite shore:
- "Remember Wisconsin!—remember your wives!
And on to your duty, boys,!—on—with your lives!'

"He turned, and he paused, as he uttered the call
Then reeled in his seat, and fell-pierced by a ball.

"He lives and he breathes yet:—the surgeons declare—
That the balance is trembling 'twixt hope and despair.
In his blanket he lies, on the hospital floor—
So calm, you might deem all his agony o'er;
And here, as I write on his face I can see
An expression whose radiance is startling to me.
His faith is sublime:—he relinquishes life,
And craves but one blessing—to look on his wife.
The Chaplain's recital is ended—no word
Frau Fan's blanched breathless lips has been heard
Till rousing herself from her passionless woe,
She simply and quietly says—"I will go."

Valley & McElhatten

There are moments of anguish so deadly, so deep,
That numbness seems over the senses to creep,
With interposition, whose timely relief
Is an anodyne-drought to the madness of grief.
Such mercy is meted to Fan; her eye
That sees as it saw not, is vacant and dry:
The billows' wild fury sweeps over her soul,
And she bends to the rush with a passive control.

Through the dusk of the night—through the glare of the day,
She urges, unconscious, her desolate way:
One image is ever her vision before;—
That blanketed form on the hospital floor!

Her journey is ended; and yonder she sees
The spot where he lies, looming white through the trees.
Her torpor dissolves with a shuddering start,
And a terrible agony clutches her heart.

The Chaplain advances to meet her:— he draws
Her silently onward;—no question—no pause;
Her finger she lays on her lips; if she spake,
She knows that the spill that upholds her, would break.

She has strength to go forward; they enter the door—
And there, on the crowded and blood-tainted floor,
Close wrapped in his blanket, lies Douglas:— his brow
Wore never a look so peaceful as now!
She stretches her arms the dear form to enfold—
God help her! -----she shrieks -----it is silent and cold!

End of poem

166

Letters to Louise Brooks

Douglas MacArthur wrote dozens of letters to Louise, most during the period of their courtship from October 1921 to the time they were married, February 14, 1922, . Twenty of these letters have been selected to illustrate the extent of Douglas's romantic prose, or because of other interesting material. A photocopy of a portion of the first letter in the series is shown below to illustrate Douglas's handwriting style.

SUPERINTENDENT'S HOUSE,
UNITED STATES MILITARY ACADEMY

My Adorable

I have

been drunk   with   the

intoxication   of   you   all

day   the   caress   of   your

eyes   the   tenderness   of

your   lips   the   sparkle

of   your   wit!   The   gleam

October 25, 1921

My Darling

How interminable the day has seemed! How perfectly colorless the crowded routine of my desk! How dismally my gray old rocks stare back at me! How insipid seem my grave professors! Where is the thrill that has always lurked within me when that thin gray line paraded? Where hides the inspiration that has armed my purpose, steeled my thoughts! Where the contentment, the calm I have known in this grim old fortress, its still life?

My papers blot out, the gray line dims into nothingness, the rocks blur into a mist—to make a halo for your head. I see only your eyes, I hear only your voice, my ears thirst for the echo of your step. Tonight my dreams will carry me far from these rock ribbed heights, away from gleaming river and sounding drum, across valley and dale, past hamlet and field, to a stately mansion, to a sacred room, and to your side, sweet Louise.

Douglas

October 27, 1921

My Adorable

I have been drunk with the intoxication of you all day. The caress of your eyes, the tenderness of your lips, the sparkle of your wit! The gleam of your smile makes my pulse shiver, the touch of your hand my head whirl, the warmth of your mouth suffocates my gasping senses and leaves me stunned and shaken with the glory and wonder of you as I enter into Paradise.

Douglas

October 28, 1921

Sweetest of Women

Your letter telling me of your Mother's visit to Washington has just come. What a thoroughbred she is! She could not be otherwise, however, and have borne such a daughter. Give her my tenderest regards and tell her I shall accept her trust in the spirit of divine love in which she makes it. I am a plain, rough soldier, more used to the camp than to the home, but such as I am, I shall love, cherish and protect my wife with the smiles, breath, tears of all my days. Tell her how I respect you, how I love you, how I trust you! Tell her that of all the honors that have come to me, of all the honors that may come to me, her gift of you will be the greatest honor of my life. Tell her my motto, "Duty, Honor, Country," reads from now on "Duty, Honor, Country, Louise." Tell her her trust is sacred and two together shall forever keep its vigil—my God and myself. I kiss your sweet lips goodnight.

Douglas

Valley & McElhatten

November 5, 1921

What a darling picture. It isn't anything like as good looking as my girl really is – but I love it. With such a one before it I can't blame the camera for keeping a little of the vision to itself – and so your picture will never quite do you justice. None but one! For in my heart is enshrined a face so fair that each drop of blood that pulses by frets with longing love as it races through my veins to come back and look again.

A week ago at this time I was losing – nothing, winning – all. The gap that separates defeat and victory is usually so narrow, but in this case would have yawned so broad, so black – just the difference for me of Death and Life. So thank you my darling, for giving me life.

Douglas

November 5 *(later)*, 1921

How adorable you were at the Cardinal's dinner! Like a queen, but queens would lack your graciousness; like an Empress, but no Empress breathes your melting imperious tenderness; like a goddess, but no goddess knows the blinding flashes of your eyes; like a fairy, but fairy fiber would fail the gossamer delicacy of your hand; like nothing in this broad world – except – how could I fail to find my word at once, - like Louise.

Douglas

November 7, 1921

My Angel Girl

I cannot tell you how disappointed I shall be Wednesday not to see you. I understand entirely, however, why you do not come and find my complete solace in the thought that you are saved fatigue and exhaustion. Though my arms will seem empty, my pulses lie still, deep within the quivering throb of my heart will lie your image. If my eyes stare vacant into nothingness it will be to see the fairy forms of divine dreams, to conjur back those golden hours of used-to-be, to live once more those poignant moments that made my world. I shall miss you—yes, but I shall dream, and those dreams the gods themselves might long to share. Are you really mine, you beautiful white soul—you passion breeding woman—you mirth making child—you tender hearted angel—you divine giver of delight—you pulsing passion flower—you exquisite atom of crystalline purity? Are you really mine? This I know. There can be no Heaven for me without you—You sweet altar of Old Fashioned Roses.

Douglas

November 8, 1921

Sweetheart

This is, by your order, to be a long letter. If I were to write really as I think it would never end, but would grow monotonous I fear as I would say and repeat and repeat incessantly the words, I love you, I love you, I love you. They compass for me the whole world but as news you would find them somewhat lacking. So, bear with me, a miserable correspondent. If I should really write you as often as I think of you my pen would never leave my hand. In everything I do you are with me. Before the eyes of the world you are about to be merged with me into one being—but spiritually and mentally it has already come to pass. I count the hours till Wednesday and live in mortal dread that you will not come. I kiss your dear eyes good night and hold you close to my heart—my own.

Douglas

The General's Women

The first paragraph of the following letter begins with a strange introspection, a recounting of the bloody uses he had turned his hands to in war, then to an uplifting of his spirit as he contemplates his forthcoming bond to Louise. The second paragraph is apparently a response to the actions of General John Pershing's efforts to derail their marriage plans.

November 15, 1921

Lovely Lady

As I write my hand with its rings *(from Louise?)* fascinates me. The hand has been with me so long, has seemed so commonplace, what strange magic on my finger changes it into a dream of wonderment? I have watched it as it fought for me on many a bloody battlefield, I have heard its trigger fingers release the leaden load, I have seen it close on more than one sinewy throat, I have felt it drive the steel home—and I have grinned at its cool readiness and skill as a killer, wondered if the day would come when it would be a second too slow—a flash too late; loved it—and thought of it no more. But today its sight thrills me as I muse on it, it seems no longer to point pistol or dirk but toward the immortal road to Paradise, its flash sweeps like a flush through my veins, and I laugh with the Gods in rapturous glee at the wonder forging those brilliant circlets that bind us together.

I am sorry the C.I.C. (Pershing) is worrying you. Sorry he is such a bully—such a blackguard as to try to blackmail you. His actions make me ashamed of the Army and as one of its senior representatives I feel like asking pardon of you for what is really impardonable. Above all things I hate cowardice in a man, and this is such a painful evidence of just that…. He is trying to break your spirit. Don't let him. If you do, you are gone. Ignore him, do not let him come to your house, do not let him telephone you, do not dance with him, do not let him speak to you except when unavoidable. Such treatment will kill him. The situation worries me not in the slightest except as it may affect you. With you beside me I am above the shafts of Fate and feel that I am at the top of the world. Love me, laugh at his vulgar villainy, and all will be well. I kiss your sweet lips with all my love.

Douglas

November 18, 1921

Darling One

I am so disappointed not to have you here this week end. I had counted so on once more being able to hear that silver voice, to see those melting eyes, to feel those tender hands. It is hard to have the cup filled up with one of loveliness alone and not be able to drink.

Are you having a wonderful time, you sparkle of loveliness, with your Lords and Ladies and Gallants Fair. Remember that when the lights fade out, the fire burns down, and all the brilliance fades into somber nothingness, with night's departing hours— that a soldier keeps your vigil at his lonely hearth with a glow within his heart that will never burn out.

Douglas

The General's Women

The letter below seems to be the aftermath of a chastisement of Louise for excessive partying, which was very much a part of her nature. Even though engaged, Louise wasn't about to forgo the pleasure of socialization. Later in the Philippines, though married, she still sought companionship when Douglas was away. What is also interesting in this letter is the role-playing as parent to child, and the suggestion of domination. There is evidence of Douglas's parent-like attitude as shown in his relationship with Isabel Cooper many years later.

November 19, 1921

Greetings, Oh Sunshine of my Life

 After listening to you call me Mr. Gloom this morning I should be more severe in my address and call you Dear Child or Dear Vamp or something equally mild—but if you could look into my heart you would know that Sunshine of my Life is really a very modest and gentle way of expressing what is there. I love you with the passions of all my life. I love you with the pure ideals of my childhood days. I love you with my smiles of Joy. I love you with my sorrow's tail (sic). I love you with each pulsing breath. I love you by Sun and by candle light. And for my love there is no surcease for as I love you more, the more I love. And so you see, I shall pester you until in self defense you yield me more and more only to find your travail deeper grown because of Love's treasures your supply is infinite—the more you give the more you have to give—and so, poor little Louise, you will be Love's Slave until death do us part.

You do not know how proud I am of you and the way you "Knock them dead." My only worry is that you will overplay and not rest enough. Eight hours for children is what the experts say, so don't cheat. Do not think for a minute I misjudge you. You are false to yourself in even considering such a possibility. You are the finest thing in this rotten old world and are above suspicion. Never let me hear you accuse yourself again by such a suggestion. Consider yourself spanked and if not up to the eight hour schedule put to bed....Good night, Destroyer of the Peace of Mind of Admirals of the Royal and Other Navies, Generals of the Army and the Army Generally, Councillors of State, and Man in General.

Douglas

The General's Women

November 21, 1921

My Darling

I have your letter of Saturday and irrespective of the merits of the case, I recognize the bruised heart it reflects and feel a flow of such sympathetic love and protection as gorges my throat and blinds my eyes. I wish more than anything in the world that I could take you in my arms and make you feel that you are the one and only love of my life. You have deluded yourself to the point where you believe it possible to compare a man's feelings toward his wife to those toward his mother. There can be no comparison. The two are things entirely different. You can no more compare them than you can day and night, black and white. They are entirely different with absolutely no point of similarity. You have no rival. You are opposing what does not exist, are building up in imagination a goblin that lacks flesh and blood. Mother loves you dearly, has welcomed you with warmest tenderness into the clan, and never by word or deed has indicated anything but the most solicitous consideration for our happiness. *(The issue of Douglas giving priority to his mother is cited later as leading to the breakup of their marriage. Despite Douglas's attempt here to portray his mother's acceptance of Louise, the evidence is much to the contrary.)*

In my present case I could not act otherwise than I did. With my dead Aunt emburied, my Mother fighting for her life from the shock that resulted, our house of sorrow should call forth only sympathy and comfort. You are my life—You mean the whole world to me—all that I am is yours—but there are some things that are not mine to give—that represent a higher *(to next page)*

177

trust than my own:—my integrity, my honor are such. Was it not that sweet gentleman Richard Lovelace who said—"I could not love you half so well, Loved I not honor more." When you speak of breaking our engagement you chill me. After Oct 21 you speak too late. In spirit and soul I have already married you. It cannot be undone.

Our mating comes of God and I cannot believe you are serious in suggesting that we not glorify such a spiritual union by a human one. On such a matter you must not joke or speak flippantly. On all others, but not, if you love me, on this one. I love you. I am wretched without you. I need you so in the time of tribulation and travail. Don't go back on me.

Douglas

November 29, 1921

Breath of Life

I am just back. To be literally truthful I should say part of me is back—and it is really a very minor part that is here. The rest remains in your gentle hands—and is thankful, grateful to be at last so truly home. The pressure of those tender fingers, the warmth of those soft palms, their sweet scent of perfume, thrills that captive trio—my heart, my soul, my spirit—with an ecstasy of shaking surrender that only those who have felt can know.
(to next page)

The General's Women

You were so true, so loyal, so like yourself to come and sit beside me Saturday at what you felt was to be a time of certain defeat. Everyone can win but it takes those like you—of real nobility, of unshakeable courage to face defeat without even the tremor of an eyelash... you came nevertheless, with never a quiver or backward glance, with your dainty feet and gossamer covering, to turn from my lips by your presence the bitter dregs of my cup, seems to me to be quite the greatest play, the ultimate height, the supremest moment of this greatest of football seasons. I have lost this year to Yale and to the Navy—and the most poignant joy I have ever known was then by you. Fate, defeat, disaster, they become mere words for me as long as you are there. I have had you this last two days to myself and those two days have completely spoiled every other day without you.

I am desolate, disconsolate, as I sit writing by my lonely log fire. How like you that fire is! Its sparkling flame, your flashing wit, its comfortable warmth the gracious gentle, geniality of your presence, its clear light the look in your eyes, its flickering flashes the curling darting tendrils of your rich brown hair, the clean tang of its smoke the fresh fragrance of your breath, its leaping crackle the rippling silver of your laugh, the drifting whiteness of its ashes the paleness flowing up from your satin breast, its steady red glow like unto nothing in this broad world but your true, loving heart. Breath of my life, forsooth, for with you I live for the first time—without you I die for the last time.

Douglas

The following letter recounts details of the ongoing issue of Douglas's reassignment. It was apparently futile despite efforts on their part to have the Secretary of War intercede. Douglas also mentions a letter from his brother Arthur, who sends congratulations on the forthcoming marriage, however, neither he nor anyone else from the family attended the wedding ceremony.

November 30, 1921

Dear Lovely Lady

My pen has started to say good night but my faltering fingers do but form I love you. All action from me, all thoughts by me, alike end in those fateful words. I love you. The oldest of all words, they have been lisped in every tongue and in every land since man and woman were, but how vibrant with new meaning they become as I whisper them to you. I had wished that I might have the skill of old scribes and masters to tell you of my love, to paint with burning phrase and glowing number the feeling in my heart, to conjur you with soft murmur of poet's fancy—to turn the ocean into ink, the land to paper, to hew the oak to make my pen, that I might truly measure to you the full feeling that burns within me—but had I all these, had I all these and more—I could not tell you more:—I love you. It is the beginning and the end, the alpha and the omega, it is all the joy, the sweetness of the world;—it is all the sanctity, all the passions of life; and if God wills after this life it is the life to come.

Douglas

December 2, 1921

My Heart

 The wind is blowing in on me as I write, stirring my paper, and singing to me of you. All things whisper of you. I hear your name in every breeze that blows and see your face in every flower. I cannot wholly lose you even when you are far away. There are violets on my table. The delicate, wholesome fragrance that clings to them makes me think of you. What beautiful thing does not? I close my eyes and put my face down to them—and you are with me. It is a kindlier power than Aladdin's lamp, for his talisman brought him nothing but gold, while mine, with unfailing tenderness, brings me the vision of you.

All day my heart has ached for you. I try not to think of those unfortunate ones who have never ever seen you and never will. It cheers me. And I console myself that no man other than I sees you in every flower—hears you in all the music that sings inside and outside his heart. There is nothing, since the day I saw you first, that is not embalmed in the amber of my memory. There is no recollection like that of loving, for love itself is a recollection, and in loving one love all the thousand memories that store themselves away.

Douglas

Valley & McElhatten

December 17, 1921

My Beautiful

Today has been so cold that I have felt like a young polar bear whose fur was not yet full grown. I believe I would freeze into a nice long icicle had I not a glow within my heart that warms and protects me from all elements. Your thought makes my pulses beat, my blood flows red, my whole being flame, no matter how the storms beat and the tempests rage.

How fine it was that your party was such as success. It could not have been otherwise, however, with you as its hostess. You have that wonderful charm, that fascinating magnetism, that marked distinction, that converts hospitality into an event, that makes entertainment seem almost a memorial. I am so proud of you!

The day has seemed long and aimless without you. All days indeed do. I keep alive by dreaming you are beside me singing softly to yourself as you so often do, and every now and then turning your face, fairer and sweeter than any flower that grows, up to mine. The brown, soft tenderness of your eyes—the ever changing music of your voice, comes to me—faint, far-off and tender, like some half-hushed lullaby. Although it will never reach you, but because it comforts my heart to give it, I send a kiss across the sleeping world to seek the scarlet haven of your laughing lips. One hundred and sixty-eight hours to Christmas.

Douglas

The General's Women

December 18, 1921

Exquisite One

The moon tonight is full and floods the earth with its gold. I grow almost faint with longing to tell you all the love of which words are too weak to carry the meaning. Last night I seemed to feel your dear arms cling. Undreamed of tenderness was in your eyes, and my soul sang in rapture such as neither bird nor flute could reach. Then you let me kiss your lips. God!—The memory of that kiss! If only the cup of slumber will give me the dream of your arms and lips, I will drain it to its dregs, and live always in your tenderness.

I have been thinking back over these last two months. Was ever such a romance in all this world before! Were we to tell the story no one would ever believe. I am no fatalist—but somehow, in this case I can but believe that God intended it so. He made us to be mates and when by accident we failed to join he intervened and brought us together. In no other way can I explain the instant love that overwhelmed me when my eyes first met yours. I cannot fail to believe that some great destiny is involved in our union and that the divine hand interposed in time to see that fate should have its way. I believe that our life together is to be one of those beautiful consecrations made in heaven and lived on earth. Its thought sanctifies me and brings to me again the feeling I had when I first partook the holy sacrament. All my life I shall love you, and glorify you with the simple, reverent trust of a great faith and passion. One hundred and forty-four days till Christmas.

Douglas

Valley & McElhatten

January 3, 1922

My Wonder Girl

I am writing again from my old desk. It groans with its load of official papers and correspondence piled up and awaiting action during my absence—but I am letting it groan. Noting seems to matter anymore but you. I find no interest in those things which have until now made my life. I get no thrill from accomplishment—I feel no irritation with its lack;—inspiration, ambition, alike seem dormant, - and I catch myself looking—looking always—backwards from these frowning hills, these freezing streams, past crowded cities and teeming towns—to where rests one who fills my waking hours, who haunts my dreams. My eyes strain, my ears thirst, my heart yearns—and my work continues to pile up.

Here in the quiet seclusion of my old haunts, I live over again the last ten days. The memory at times almost suffocates me. I can feel the white in my cheeks—the shake in my knees—the gasp in my throat—when visions of you flash before me. How completely you have changed my world and faintly realize. You have lifted me to a delirium of joy, an ecstasy of bliss, the very existence of which was unknown. I have felt before the heaven of your presence, but never, never did I dream of the wonder as you are. The mere thought makes me faint and sick.

Mother was delighted beyond words with your "barbershop" effort. She said you seemed to have turned the clock back ten years for me. Will you turn it back tens years in other things? Time flies so fast with you beside me that those ten years would but seem to fill the gaps of the fleeing hours that steal away on unknown wing when you are by. Ten years with you is but a breath. Ten years without you would make Time himself seem old.

Douglas

The General's Women

January 12, 1922

My Beloved

I am back, lonely, desolate, sick at heart for you. Although the drums still beat, the bugles blow, without your voice a silence hangs in the air like that of lonely graveyards. The sun still shines, but without your eyes a blackness swims before me like deepest night. My boys in gray still laugh and frolic, but without my Playmate I am gripped by the desolation of an utter misery.

Again it has been a week we have been together and how intensified, how cemented, have the days made the ties that bind us! You have been wonderful, Ray of Sunshine, and have touched my dear old post with a glory that clings to every nook and corner.

How the snow would tempt me if you were only here to tramp the trails beyond Fort Pitt, but how it sickens me to think of climbing them without you. With you nothing becomes everything—without you everything would be nothing. I am holding the mail to send this line which though necessarily short in length is weighted with such a deep love as passeth human understanding.

Douglas

January 17, 1922

My Own Darling

 I am working like a beaver cheered on by the vision of your dear face before me, the echo of your soft voice about me, the memory of your warm arms around me. It is really but a few fleeting hours since we were together but it seems like ages. How wonderful will be the time when I do not have to watch either the calendar or the clock to measure when I shall see you. How beautiful to live those charming lines—"two souls with but a single thought, two hearts that beat as one."

As I look back upon my life it seems like an old fashioned garden of years in which I have planted Hope and there sprang up Despair, and many things I thought would bring me bloom and sweetness only stung and burned. I wanted only beauty and fragrance and there came up thorns. I made the paths smooth and even on the morrow they were overgrown with weeds and brambles. Alien hands interfered with my sowing and dropped strange seeds in the ground. The weeds thrive and the flowers died, and where I planted roses, there came up nettles. But in spite of weeds and thorns there is at least one spot of beauty in my garden that fills me with joy. When I am tired I turn to it and the sight refreshes me. It is a single flower and is always in bloom. It is a tall, stately lily, white and sweet and fair, and so divinely fragrant that you know before I say what it is—My love for you.

Douglas

End of book